Dead Birds
Singing

Dead Birds
Singing

MARC TALBERT

Little, Brown and Company
BOSTON   TORONTO

FIRST EDITION

Library of Congress Cataloging in Publication Data

Talbert, Marc, 1953 —
    Dead birds singing.

    Summary: After his mother is killed and his sister
is badly injured in a car accident, seventh-grader
Matt faces life with a new family and a deep feeling of
anger.
    [1. Death — Fiction]   I. Title.
PZ7.T14145De   1985   [Fic]   85-147
ISBN 0-316-83125-5

BP

*Published simultaneously in Canada
by Little, Brown & Company (Canada) Limited*

PRINTED IN THE UNITED STATES OF AMERICA

For Moo
Through whose eyes
I see the world
Anew each day

Dead Birds
Singing

One

*U*nmistakable. *Through the echoes, shouts, and confusion in the swimming pool* Matt heard his name. It was shouted so loudly he was sure everybody would be stunned into silence. But the pool room noise continued, louder than before.

"Matt!" He heard it again. It sounded like Jeannie, his older sister, yelling at the top of her lungs. Without looking up at the stands, Matt pictured his sister yelling, twirling her red sweater over her head like a lasso, jumping up and down, generally making a fool of herself — like always. Next to her Matt pictured his mother, sitting quietly, perhaps reading a book, trying to look unrelated to the screaming maniac next to her.

Matt sighed. Probably all the friends and family of the five teams competing in the junior regional swim meet were staring at his sister and trying to figure out who she belonged to.

"Matt!" Again his name echoed through the building.

"I think someone's trying to get your attention," said Jamie, who was sitting next to Matt against the tile wall under the stands facing the pool. Jamie was shivering slightly, even though he was wrapped up in a huge blue thick towel that matched his racing suit. "Your girlfriend?" he asked.

"No," Matt said.

"Your wife?"

Matt elbowed Jamie, knocking him over on his side. Jamie, all curled up, tried to get up without unwrapping himself.

"Help," Jamie said, his laughter muffled by the folds of his towel. His feet stuck out at ridiculous ducklike angles. "I'm being attacked by a towel!"

Matt laughed and reached over to his friend. In his best Coach Woodbury imitation he said, "Oh dry up! I wish you were as coordinated as your swimsuit and your towel!" He pulled Jamie upright. Jamie was grinning, red in the face.

"Matt!" The voice rang out again.

"What a mouth," Matt muttered. He turned around and looked up and behind, into the stands. His jaw dropped a notch when he saw who was yelling at him.

His mother wasn't swinging a sweater over her head or jumping up and down. But as soon as she saw him looking up she waved frantically and smiled. Next to her was Jeannie, sitting at a slight angle away from her mother, staring at the ceiling, determined not to be associated with the crazy lady next to her.

Now that she had his attention, Matt's mother reached down and held up a little paper sack.

"Oranges?" she mouthed, pointed to the sack.

"Do you want an orange, Jamie?" Matt asked, barely moving his lips, flashing a forced smile up at his mother.

"No."

"Neither do I." Matt shrugged his shoulders and shook his head slightly from side to side. His mother smiled back and sat down, looking as if nothing had happened.

Jeannie shot her mother a withering look of disgust. I wonder what she'll write about Mom in her diary tonight, Matt thought.

Matt turned around and sat down. Just as he was comfortable Matt heard his coach yell, "All right, team. Let's have a powwow."

They gathered their towels around themselves and walked stiffly over to the knot of shivering, half-naked boys that made up the team. In the middle of this knot, clipboard in hand, was Coach Woodbury, his bald head damp with the dew of excitement.

"His head's shiny enough to blind a seeing eye dog," muttered Matt. "Should be a law against it."

"He's not *that* bright," Jamie replied.

"OK, men," Coach Woodbury began.

"Men?" Jamie whispered, looking around. "I don't see any chest hair. I don't even see any pimples."

"This is the last meet of a season we're all proud of." The coach's voice cracked on the last word and he cleared his throat. "I want you to know that regardless of how we do, I consider you a swell bunch of swimmers." He looked around the group of boys. "You know your events. Just swim strong and relaxed. I know you'll do your best."

He looked down at his roster. "Any questions? Good. Go out and swim right out of your suits!"

"Not me!" Matt said. "I swim the backstroke!" The team laughed. Coach Woodbury smiled.

"Nobody would notice anyway," Jamie said. "You're not

5

exactly Moby Dick." Matt's smile disappeared as everybody laughed. Sometimes he wanted to punch his best friend in the kisser — knock a little sense into him that didn't have anything to do with humor.

As he walked back to his spot against the wall, Matt thought of the pool that morning when they first arrived. The others were in the locker room changing and running around when Matt walked into the pool room. The smell of the chlorine made his stomach tighten. The smooth surface of the pool reflected the ceiling lights in bright patches. The water moved up and down gently, as if it was breathing. It looked very cold as Matt knelt down by the pool's edge and dipped his hand in. Surprisingly the water was warm, but a wave of goose bumps made him shiver.

Now the water was alive. It seemed angry. The smell of chlorine mingled with the smell of wet, sweating bodies. The red bob-line dividing the lanes rode the bucking waves. The bleary black lane stripes on the pool's bottom slid in and out of view. And the water swarmed with pale thin bodies in yellow, green, purple, blue, and orange racing suits.

He looked at the water and remembered something his mother had said as they drove to the meet. "And just to think" — she beamed, looking over her shoulder — "you couldn't float or swim at all two years ago."

It was true. For as long as he could remember, one of Matt's biggest fears had been of the water. "You're so afraid of water you don't even like to eat *fish!*" Jeannie sometimes taunted. Three Christmases ago she'd given him a fishbowl.

"If you don't like water, fill it with dirt and plants," she'd joked.

That was the last straw. He was both angry and humiliated about having a fear his sister could bug him about. So Matt had signed up for swimming lessons the next week.

The lessons weren't easy. He was almost twice as old as any other kid in the class. Because of his age, the teacher expected him to help the littler ones float and kick in water that lapped at his shoulders and sloshed onto his face and stung his eyes. Once he slipped, and the water swallowed him up. The boy he was helping merrily floated and kicked above him. Matt scrambled to regain his footing and, finally, punched his head through the water's surface and into the air, gasping. That had been embarrassing. But the embarrassment of not being able to dive in front of the little kids had almost killed him.

During the lessons, Matt not only learned to swim; he discovered he was good at it. Very good, in fact. He had tamed the water. He celebrated by getting goldfish for the fishbowl Jeannie had given him.

But his respect for the water was like the respect for an old bully he beat up when he was five. Let your defenses down once, turn your back at the wrong time and — wham! Regardless of how much he swam, Matt still felt that way — a combination of pride and fear, joy and dread.

Matt stretched his legs and shoulders and watched the meet unfold. Each swimmer had a pre-race ritual — a different way to shake the jitters from his arms and legs, a different way to breathe deeply and to prepare mentally for competition.

Many of the boys, including Jamie, looked pale and scared.

Their lips were blue and their eyes were bloodshot and haunting. Some were shivering uncontrollably and some were almost unable to move from where they were plopped.

Others, like Jamie, couldn't stop talking. As Matt helped Jamie stretch before his freestyle event — pulling Jamie's shoulders loose — he half listened.

"They look mean," Jamie chattered. "Big and mean. I'll have to swim like a shark's after me. Look at that guy over there with the biceps as big and hairy as his head! Looks dumb but I bet he can swim. Have to swim like a shark's after me, all right. Big shark with rows of teeth with hair and clothes and guts hanging out of his mouth."

He chattered on and Matt just listened, grunting now and then. The voice of the sound system announced Jamie's event.

"Good luck," Matt said, slapping Jamie on the rear. "Watch out for sharks!"

"Big and mean, boy. Gotta swim strong," Jamie muttered as he stepped on the starting block. His head was bowed, his brow was puckered, his mouth was pulled tight and grim. He looked like he was stepping up to an executioner's chopping block. Matt could detect in his own mouth the metallic taste that was probably flavoring Jamie's saliva. It made Matt feel like he was sucking on a nail.

The gun fired and Matt watched his friend start swimming frantically before he even hit the water. He looked like an eggbeater — trying to make whipped cream out of water. Matt smiled. Water flew in every direction.

He's digging a hole in the water, Matt thought, one that keeps filling up. Swimming is kind of like that. But it's more like digging a tunnel. You grab a hunk of water in front of you and hurl it at your feet. You kick it behind you as you grab another hunk of water.....

If Jamie would only relax, Matt thought, calm down and think, he wouldn't be such an eggbeater. Matt watched as Jamie struggled through four laps for a last-place showing. As Matt helped him out of the pool and handed him a towel, he peered down at Jamie's feet.

"Better count those toes," he said. "Shark may have nabbed a couple."

Jamie was drained but relieved that the race was over. "I felt something tugging at my suit, and it wasn't the water rushing by," he said, shakily.

"Probably a shark trying to decide if you were suitable or not," Matt said.

Jamie smiled weakly and sat down. "Good luck. Hope you do better than I did."

Matt's event was next. The score on the board looked bad. Even if his teammates won or placed in the rest of the events, they'd still lose big. But, Matt thought as he walked up to the pool, I'd sure like to end the season with a win.

"Yeah, Matt!" he heard from the stands. He looked up and saw his sister jumping up and down, waving her sweater. She was twirling it around her head like a lasso. Matt laughed and waved. His mother, trying to pull Jeannie back into her seat, smiled weakly and waved at Matt with her free hand.

"This is the worst part," Matt muttered, slipping into the water. It was cool but not cold, and he quickly dunked his head under. Magically, the sound and confusion of the pool room were swallowed up in watery stillness.

9

Matt let his breath out slowly and followed the bubbles to the surface. His head popped above the water and he was hit by an explosion of noise.

He looked up and down the lanes of the pool, sizing up the competition. Right next to him, in lane number three, was a guy who looked big enough to be in ninth grade. He was staring at Matt, and as soon as Matt looked in his direction, the guy reached over the bob-line, hand extended.

"I'm Fred," he said, stony-faced.

Matt stuck out his hand and winced as Fred grabbed it and squeezed hard. "I'm Matt."

"No," Fred said, never taking his eyes off Matt, "you're slow. I'm gonna whip your butt, sucker."

He must have flunked seventh grade three or four times, Matt thought, narrowing his eyes to slits. "We'll see," Matt replied, pulling his hand away. He dipped his head under again, calming himself. Once more the noise was swallowed up — except for the pounding in his ears. "I'm going to win, I'm going to win," he thought.

Matt pushed from the bottom. He shot into the world of light and noise and movement and grabbed the handles of the starting block.

"Judges and timers ready," the starter shouted. "Swimmers, take your marks. . . ." Matt pulled himself up so that only the tip of his rear touched the water. The room was suddenly still.

BANG! Matt pushed off, grunting, arching his back and throwing his arms over his head. He began to kick strongly and his arms moved smoothly through the water. He breathed deeply, concentrating on good form — strong, even strokes — and the row of ceiling lights.

Flags appeared overhead, and he prepared to flip turn, dipping his left shoulder and throwing his legs over. Perfect. As his face broke the surface, he looked at his feet and saw the guy in number three just beginning his turn.

Matt felt an exhilarating surge of energy. The water rushed past his ears and his breathing came a little quicker, steady and deep. He picked up his pace and kept rhythm to a chant in his head: "I'm ahead. I'm ahead. I'm ahead."

A perfect turn at the other end, and he could see Jamie and his teammates yelling and jumping up and down. He couldn't hear them, but Jamie held up a finger.

"I'm number one." The chant changed and shifted into high gear. His arms were heavier now. His legs were a little lower in the water. He grimaced, saw the flags, flipped, and, with a mighty push, launched himself into the final lap.

Time seemed to slow down. He blocked out everything, closed his eyes, and concentrated on each stroke. "I'm number one. I'm number one." Amid the chant he suddenly felt the wall with the tips of his right fingers and brought his knees to his chest so that he would stop gliding before he banged his head. As he stood up in his lane, gasping, the sound of cheering washed over him like a huge, breaking wave. Jamie's face was red, and he was kneeling along the edge. "You won! You won!"

Matt closed his eyes, leaned back, and floated to shut out the sounds and to catch his breath.

It felt good to win.

Two

 att stretched out and snuggled into the length of the back seat of the car and listened to the tires on the pavement. It sounded like a continuous strip of Velcro ripping apart — only muffled.

The rest of the swim meet seemed dreamy and unreal, like he'd observed it through goggles that were half-filled with water. In fact, Matt had been in such a daze that he didn't even shower or take off his wet suit before throwing on his clothes and parka. The clingy suit pinched and tugged at his crotch. He reached down and pulled at it under his jeans, rearranging himself.

Over the soothing wind, like dry lips whistling, and the windshield wipers swatting at heavy, thick snow, Matt listened to his mother and sister talk.

"That was an awfully exciting race," his mother gushed. "I don't know when I've been more excited."

"You couldn't have embarrassed me more," Jeannie snapped. "Jumping up and down, screaming and yelling, and, I couldn't believe it, you were crying, for crying out loud!"

"Oh hush. I just don't know when I've been more excited." His mother paused. "This snow is pretty bad and the road's getting slick."

"You didn't have to act like a *complete* idiot. People were staring...."

"At *you,* most likely," his mother retorted. "You were *much* louder than I was when you were telling *me* to be quiet!" She peered over her right shoulder and, in a quieter voice, asked, "Matt, how do you feel?"

"Fine, Mom. Just feel like I've swum the English Channel."

"Well, I'm proud of you, son, real proud. I just wish your father could have seen you."

Matt's mother hardly ever mentioned his father, except when she was very happy or very sad. His father had been killed in the war right before Matt was born. She always told him that he looked like his father. Sometimes, when Matt looked at old pictures of his father, he could see himself. It gave him the creeps.

Jeannie's body suddenly stiffened and her voice became shrill. "Watch out, Mom. That guy's coming right at us!"

His mother gasped and slammed on the brakes. Matt was jerked farther into the folds of the back seat. "Oh my God!" The car slid sideways, and Matt's mother frantically turned the steering wheel, first left and then right, shoving him feet-first toward one door and then headfirst toward the other. His mother's voice rose to a scream. "No! NO!"

Matt tried to scramble up onto his hands and knees to see what was happening. A violent explosion of crunching metal, shattering glass, and Matt was hurled, shoulder-first, into the back of the front seat. Pain overwhelmed him and he blacked out.

Matt heard frantic voices. They seemed far away. He slowly opened his eyes. A blue light was flashing, in rhythm to the throbbing in his shoulder and head. The voices gradually became louder and clearer. They were right outside the car.

"Quick, check out the girl." The voice was gruff.

"She's breathing, sort of." The second voice was shaky and on the other side of the car. "What a mess."

"There's a kid in the back. See if he's all right," ordered the first voice.

The door by his head grated as it was pried open. Matt felt as if he was in a giant tin can that someone was trying to stab open with a knife. He closed his eyes as a flashlight passed over his face.

"Out cold. Looks OK," said the second voice. Matt heard the wail of a siren. "Ambulance coming," the first man shouted. "Rip the door off — driver's side front!"

Matt lay, cringing, in the swirl of nightmare sensations — the flashing lights, the siren, the smell of gas and oil, the sound of metal grinding metal as someone pried open the door.

The ambulance slid to a halt and doors slammed.

"Quick, get that girl on plasma," a strong voice ordered.

Even though his eyes were shut, Matt saw a beam pass over his face. "Get this boy out! Stretcher! Get the boy!"

Another voice. "Woman's out. Check on her, quick! Goddamn it, get this man out of the way!"

Matt felt strong, gentle hands lift him from the floor

14

between the front and rear seats. He felt as if he floated onto the stretcher, where he was carefully placed on his back. Gentle hands opened each eyelid and flashed a soft light into each one.

"Get him inside!"

As the stretcher moved, Matt turned his head and looked toward the blinking confusion around the car. In the flashing light and the globs of snow falling from the sky the windshield seemed to be a spiderweb of cracks radiating from a dark, gaping hole on the passenger side. On the hood his sister sprawled, one cheek on the hood, facing him, eyes closed. Her face was horribly mangled. Blood oozed and dropped from her face and mouth down the side of the car into a growing patch of bright red snow. A man in a down parka was slowly turning her upward, and he began sticking a tube down into her mouth.

Matt could barely see the shape of his mother through the hole. A shadow moved about her slumped figure. Another ambulance drove up and stopped behind their car. Its lights flashed as two people got out. Where's the noise? Matt wondered. Lights were flashing, people were moving, and snow was falling. It looked like TV with the sound down low.

Maybe I've gone deaf, Matt thought. He tried to get up, but the straps held him down, and he heard a voice above him. "Steady, kid. Relax. You're gonna be all right." A heavy snowflake hit below his eyes and slid down his cheek like a tear.

Suddenly someone grabbed his arm. Matt's eyes flew open and he looked up into a man's face, cut above the eye, tears and blood streaming down his face.

"I sho shorry," the man blubbered.

"Get this idiot out of here!" someone yelled.

Matt closed his eyes tightly and shut out what he'd seen. He was lifted inside, and the ambulance pulled away.

Again and again and again, the siren seared through his aching head. Each time an image burned to life in his mind — his sister on the hood, face down, blowing big red bubbles, stupidly making motor noises.

Out of the jagged hole in the windshield came a man's voice. It blended with sounds like fingernails clawing a chalkboard, sending shivers up Matt's spine. "I sho shorry. I sho shorry. I sho shorry."

Matt suddenly realized who had smashed into them. "Son of a bitch!" he yelled, clenching his fists. "Son of a bitch!" A hand soothed his forehead. Matt clenched his fists tighter and, drowning in a wave of pain, he fainted again.

Three

*M*att felt something on his left shoulder, like a spider crawling toward his head. He reached up with his right hand to flick it off and, instead, he touched a hand.

His eyes flew open. He jerked his head to the side and, at the same time, struggled to sit up. He was startled to see a nurse hovering above him, adjusting a sling which held his left arm against his ribs. Matt realized he wasn't wearing a shirt. He was lying on an examining table that was covered with a strip of white paper that crinkled when he moved.

Matt looked down at his feet. His pants and socks and shoes were also missing. The only thing he was wearing was his swimsuit, which had been untied and loosened around his waist.

"Lie back, now," the nurse said, gently but firmly pushing him back to the table with one hand. Her other hand cupped the back of his head, keeping it from hitting the pillow too hard. Her voice was surprisingly low and rough. "Just sit back while I call for the doctor. He wants to see you."

Matt's eyes darted around the bright white room with its gleaming instruments arranged on the counters and walls and the smell of alcohol swabs and adhesive tape. In a panic now, he remembered the accident — almost felt the jolt in the pit of his stomach.

"Need some help over here!" He heard a voice right outside the door to his room. A cart with a huge cylinder and hoses clanked by, pushed by a person wearing a gauze mask and dressed in a green pajamalike suit.

"Hurry up. Pressure's almost zero." The voice was urgent. A nurse ran by, followed closely by a tall man with a stethoscope flung over his shoulder, flopping against his back.

Matt tried to shut out the noise and confusion by squeezing his eyes closed. Images flashed in his mind, conjured up by the sounds outside — blood dripping, scalpels gleaming, machines pumping and sucking, faceless people in white masks running in all directions and yelling. Matt cringed and gritted his teeth. To stop the nightmare raging in his head, he forced his eyes open.

In the doorway he saw Jamie's mother, Judy. Her face was twisted into a grimace. She was fighting back tears — and losing. Her cheeks were streaked where tears dribbled down, washing away makeup. Her hands were clasped in front of her. She was clutching a purse.

"Hi, Matt," she said. Her voice was raspy, like carrots being grated. She walked stiffly into the room and sat gingerly in a chair next to Matt's head. Letting go of her purse, she reached toward Matt and grasped his right hand, which hadn't moved from his stomach since it reached up to flick off the imagined spider. Judy's grip was tight — too tight — and it was trembly.

She looked at him for a couple of moments, fighting for control of her face. She cleared her throat.

"Matt." Her voice shook. "We weren't too far behind you when you crashed — " she gulped some air and struggled to control the quake in her voice — "when the accident happened. As soon as I took Jamie home I came over." Tears welled up in her eyes. Her grip tightened until Matt's arm hurt.

"Matt, I have something terrible to tell you. Your mother is dead." Tears spilled over and streamed down her stricken face.

Matt felt a cry build in his gut, sucking the air from his lungs. His head rang and his ears buzzed. What did she say? He shuddered. It wasn't true! It was a lie! It was a mistake. His mother was hurt. But she would get better. Matt's face scrunched and, gasping for air, he blurted, "NO!"

He was angry — and shocked. How could she say such a thing! He looked in disbelief at Judy's face and his mind raced with questions. How could his mother be dead? Hadn't he heard her voice and talked to her? Couldn't he hear her now?

"Dr. Woods, please come to emergency. Please come to emergency, Dr. Woods." There! Over the loudspeaker! That was his mother's voice! He could hear it, plain as anything. He stared at Judy. She *must* have heard it too. He watched for a flicker of recognition in her face — some signal that she had heard his mother's voice.

"Matt," she repeated. "Your mother is *dead*." Again she fought back tears.

Dead? The word sounded heavy and grim — like a foul ball hitting the roof of a car. Or like a head bouncing off the hood of a car. He winced. Dead. His mother, dead?

Matt heard the voice again, more mechanical and almost lifeless. "Dr. Woods, please come to emergency." It no longer sounded like his mother's. The voice was drowned out by noises of people walking quickly past his door.

Matt couldn't take his eyes off Judy's face. "No," he said. His voice was weak. A clammy feeling began to spread from his head to the rest of his body. Tears ran down Judy's face, and her nose began to drip. She pressed her lips lightly together and nodded her head yes.

"No?" Matt tried one more time to convince her that it was a terrible joke. Again she nodded her head.

The clammy feeling intensified. His head seemed to float above the pillow. His legs seemed to melt into the table and his arms completely disappeared. Sounds faded and the light dimmed.

Judy, sobbing now, half stood. Her purse fell to the floor with a thud. She reached over and gathered Matt awkwardly into her arms. Her tears dripped onto his head. Slowly the noise outside the room grew louder and the lights above him brightened. Matt could faintly feel his legs.

A shadow blocked some of the light overhead and Matt looked up from Judy's bosom to see a tall, thin man with glasses, standing over Judy. The man gently put a hand on her shoulder and shook her softly. Startled, Judy choked in mid-sob and looked up and over her shoulder. The man stepped around toward Matt and helped Judy arrange Matt back on the table.

"Mrs. Fletcher, I'm Dr. Woods. I'd like to talk with Matt for a couple of minutes." He turned to face Matt.

Judy started to get to her feet. Without looking away from Matt, Dr. Woods signaled with his hand that she should stay.

"Matt, I have some sad things to tell you." His tone of voice was sad, yet matter-of-fact. Matt watched his face. It looked tired, and little bags sagged under his eyes. "Your mother is dead."

Matt stared at the doctor. That word again. *Dead.* "She was killed instantly in the crash." He paused. "Your sister is in an operating room. Her leg is hurt very badly." Dr. Woods seemed to be studying Matt, looking for reactions to what he was saying. Matt's expression was blank, unchanged.

Dr. Woods turned to Judy. "Who will be looking out for Matt?" he asked.

Judy swallowed hard. "We will."

"I would like to keep Matt here overnight," Dr. Woods said. He walked around the table and faced Judy and Matt. Reaching down, he felt Matt's bandaged arm and shoulder. "I don't think he'll need this more than a day or two." He looked at Matt's head. "You got quite a knock on the noodle," he said. He looked at Judy. "His concussion is mild. But we should keep him overnight for observation." He continued to knead Matt's arm and shoulder. Matt winced a couple of times when Dr. Woods hit sore spots.

Dr. Woods stood up. "Matt, you need some rest. The

nurse will be in here soon to give you something to help you sleep." He turned to Judy. "I'd like to talk with you about a few things, Mrs. Fletcher."

Judy stood up, looking like a child expecting a scolding. She looked at Dr. Woods and then she looked over at Matt. "Try to get some rest, Matt," she said quietly. "I'll be back for you tomorrow."

They turned and walked out the door. Almost immediately a nurse bustled in. She was the nurse who had startled Matt earlier. Without saying a word, she wrapped a cuff around his good arm and plugged the ends of a stethoscope into her ears. "Gonna take your blood pressure," she said, and she began pumping up the cuff. Matt's heart beat faster as the cuff constricted around his arm. The nurse concentrated on her watch and slowly let air out. "Good for you," she said.

She took the cuff off. "Let me check those baby blues." She lifted each of Matt's eyelids with her thumb and stared a few moments at each widened eye. "Those peepers look pretty good," she said. She smiled. "I'll be back in a bit." The nurse bustled out.

Matt closed his eyes. Faint smells of vomit and urine and poop occasionally overpowered the smell of disinfectant and seeped into the room. And people scurried by the door.

Just as Matt was drifting off, he felt a breeze in the room. He opened his eyes. The nurse was standing next to him with a greenish piece of cloth in one hand and a glass of water in the other. She grinned and put the glass on a table next to his bed. She pulled out a small envelope of pills from a pocket in her uniform and put them next to the glass. "These will help you sleep," she said in her rough voice. She lifted up the greenish cloth with both hands and it fell into the familiar shape of a pajama top. "And these are your 'jammies,'" she said. "Not the prettiest in the world, but they'll be dry and comfortable."

She helped him sit up and swing his feet around. "Not dizzy now, are you?" she asked, pinching her face together and looking at him. Matt felt slightly faint but shook his head. "Good," she said. "Let me help you stand." Her breath smelled strongly of tobacco.

Matt reached for the floor with his toes and slid off the examining table. Almost as soon as his feet touched the floor, his swimsuit skidded down his legs and settled around his ankles. Matt looked in surprise at his crotch and reached with his good hand to cover himself up.

"No need for that," the nurse said. "I knew you were a boy all along. And believe me, it's nothing to be ashamed of." She popped the pajama top over Matt's head. "Stick your arm up here. Promise I won't look."

Matt hesitated and then quickly jabbed his good arm where he thought the armhole should be. His arm shot through the head hole instead, and he brought it down and jabbed again.

"There," the nurse said, pulling the rest of the top down. It went halfway to his knees. "We'll leave the other arm inside. Let's sit down." She reached beside the door and rolled a wheelchair toward Matt. He stared at it, dumbly. His head began to throb. He'd never sat in a wheelchair before. "Come on," the nurse said. "I'm a safe driver." He stepped out of his swimsuit and she helped him sit down. The pajamas rode up over his bottom to the small of his back. The vinyl of the wheelchair felt cold. "Before we go, take these," the nurse said. "They'll help you sleep."

Matt felt drowsy as they went down corridor after corridor, turning right and left and left and right. They got in an elevator and Matt couldn't tell if they went up or down.

Finally the nurse wheeled him into a room and up to a bed. She pulled down the blankets and helped him stand and get in. "This is a buzzer for the night nurse," she said, pointing to a button on the wall above his head. A little red light, the size of the head of a match, shone right below it. Matt could barely keep his eyes open. "Don't hesitate to call. Goodnight now," she said, pulling the covers up to his chin.

Matt did not want to sleep. He was afraid he would never wake up. But before he knew it, he fell into a hard, dreamless sleep.

Matt woke slowly. A headache had been growing from the back of his eyes. He felt like the morning after he and Jamie had split a six-pack of beer. He kept his eyes closed, remembering how light made his headache worse that morning after.

Slowly Matt realized where he was. He heard people walking back and forth outside the room. He was startled to hear the creak of a mattress next to him and a deep voice mutter, "Damn it. Where are my glasses? Can't see a damn thing, damn it."

Matt held his breath and listened. He opened his eyes and turned his head. A curtain separated his bed from the one next to him. Just then Dr. Woods walked in, followed by a stern-looking nurse.

"Good morning, Matt," Dr. Woods said. "Glad to see you're awake. How do you feel?"

"Hey!" the deep voice sounded from the other side of the curtain. "Could somebody kindly help a sick man find his glasses?" The nurse looked at Dr. Woods, who nodded. She walked briskly behind the curtain. "Thanks," the deep voice muttered. The nurse came back. "You're not bad-looking now that I can see," he called after her.

Matt sat up and Dr. Woods pulled the pajama top up and over his taped shoulder. Matt clutched the sheets to his waist to hide his nakedness. Dr. Woods silently checked Matt over, very much like the day before. He scribbled occasionally on a clipboard the nurse handed him every time he stuck his hand out toward her.

"You look good," Dr. Woods finally said, standing up. He smiled slightly.

"How's Jeannie?" Matt asked.

The smile disappeared from Dr. Wood's face. "She's recovering now from her operation," he said. "I'll go check on her a little later and let you know how she's doing." He turned and left.

Time sometimes seemed to speed up to Matt — like a train, whistle blowing, coming at him. At other times time seemed to slow down — like a train racing away. The morning went by and Matt slept on and off, wakened only by nurses who came in to check on him, or by the voice next to him complaining about something or other.

Matt pretended that everything was all right — that his

mother was fine and his sister OK. Lunch came and went and Matt felt an urge building to go to the bathroom.

Matt screwed up his courage and, turning toward the curtain, said, "Hey! Where's the bathroom."

He held his breath and listened. The room was still. He jumped when the gruff voice broke the stillness. "Name's not 'Hey.' It's Bert, and the bathroom's behind the door where your feet are pointed. Just don't let the nurse catch you using it by yourself."

"But I gotta go," Matt said, timidly.

"I won't tell," said Bert. Matt heard him shift his weight on his bed. "Wish I could go, but I can't," Bert said. "Have to get hooked up to a catheter. Means I just watch a little jug fill up with my pee until my bladder's empty." Matt heard Bert's bed groan again. "I'm getting better, though. I know it. When I look at that jug filling up with pee and pee foam, I think of beer." Bert laughed so hard he started to cough. "It'll sure . . . feel good to . . . pee . . . on my own . . . soon," he gasped.

Matt didn't know what to say. Why was this guy Bert telling him this? What was a catheter, anyway? Matt thought vaguely of a tube sticking up his . . . He shook his head. That was just too gross to think about.

Just as Matt was about to sit on the edge of his bed, Judy walked in, followed by a nurse. The nurse was holding his shirt, pants, and coat in one hand and his shoes and socks in the other.

"Dr. Woods thinks you can go now," Judy said, smiling. She looked tired. "Oh." She reached into her purse and fumbled around. "They told me you might want some undies, so I brought you a pair of Jamie's."

26

The nurse helped him sit up and swing his feet around. "Reach for the stars, partner," she said, playfully. "This is a stickup." Matt reached up, and the nurse pulled off his pajama tops. She quickly draped the shirt over his shoulders. "Let's get this good arm in the sleeve," she said. "That's a trooper. Now stick your feet in these." She held out the underpants and Matt stepped into them. She shoved them up to above his knees. "OK, let's stand up." The nurse helped him stand and she pulled the underpants up, snapping the elastic against the skin on each side of his waist. "OK, now these." She held out his pants, and Matt meekly stuck his feet in both pant legs. The nurse pulled them up, zipping and buttoning them in one motion.

"Thanks," said Judy as the nurse draped Matt's parka around his shoulders. "Thanks a lot."

"Take care now," the nurse called over her shoulder as she began stripping the bed. Matt watched.

"Let's go, Matt," Judy said, trying to shepherd him toward the door.

The nurse turned around, surprised that they were still there. She looked down at Matt's feet. She smiled, and her sagging cheeks lifted like a raised theater curtain. "Forgot your shoes, didn't we?" She walked over and sat him down in a chair by the door. She fetched the shoes and put them on and tied them nimbly.

Matt looked at Judy and then at the nurse.

"Can I wait here?" he asked quietly.

The nurse's smile disappeared and the skin, like a curtain, dropped. "Whatever for, dear?" she asked.

"For Jeannie," Matt said.

27

Judy sucked in a breath and walked over to Matt. "Jeannie's hurt very badly, Matt."

"That's right," the nurse said. "She was hurt pretty badly and you need to get home and get some sleep."

Matt stood up slowly. Suddenly he couldn't concentrate and his brain felt numb. "Hurt pretty badly." That's what everybody was saying. How badly was Jeannie hurt? Where? Why don't they tell me more? Why can't I see her? Where is Dr. Woods? He promised to let me know.

Questions fluttered from his half-opened mouth and disappeared silently like birds from a cage.

"So long, kid. Take care." Bert's voice rang out as they walked out the door. "Didn't hear the toilet flush."

Matt suddenly remembered that he had to go. "May I?" he asked, nodding his head toward the bathroom door. Judy nodded back.

"Here," the nurse said, reaching over and unzipping his pants. "That should help."

That's weird, Matt thought as he stood above the toilet. I never saw Bert once. I wonder what he looks like? I wonder why he's here? Nothing was coming, so Matt held his breath and concentrated. He certainly didn't want to be hooked up to a catheter, whatever that was.

Four

he ride to the Fletchers' home was terrifying. Matt insisted that Judy buckle him in and that she lock all the doors. He was tense. He peered out the windshield at oncoming traffic, gritting his teeth, not wanting to look but unable to keep his eyes off the road. At any moment he expected a car to slide out of control in front of them on the slushy road.

Judy was nervous too. Her stops were abrupt, her starts sudden and she overreacted to cars coming at her or passing her — which happened often because she was driving painfully slowly.

Neither of them said a word.

The snow of the day before had stopped. The late afternoon was fading into dusk. They turned off a busy main street into the Fletchers' neighborhood. Cars were parked under the snow-shrouded branches of the trees, each car blanketed by snow and brightly lit from above by the streetlights.

Slightly hypnotized by the regular, rhythmic passing of these cars, Matt no longer felt the moving sensation of the car he was in. As he looked out the window he saw a ghostly procession of cars moving past him, backward, into the dark.

He started, snapping his head to the front. Judy turned the last corner and into the driveway.

As they drove toward the large brick colonial-style house, framed by big bushes and sheltered by old trees, Matt saw light streaming from every window.

Judy parked the car next to the sidewalk leading to the back door and kitchen. "Stay put," she said, climbing out of the car. But Matt had his door open before she reached his side.

"Let me help you," she said, steadying Matt as he stood up. Cold air slipped through the gaps of his half-buttoned shirt and coat, making him shiver. He was a little stiff as he walked arm in arm with Judy. The sidewalk had been hastily shoveled, and Matt stepped gingerly over missed globs of snow.

Just as Judy reached for the knob, the door flew open. There in the doorway stood Jamie. He looked awkward, like he had to go to the bathroom and didn't know where.

"Do you have a reservation?" Jamie asked, his face splitting into a smirk. "I'd have lots of reservations if I came to a place like this." He snickered nervously and, more soberly, said, "Let me help you." Jamie grasped the elbow of Matt's taped arm and pulled.

"Ouch!" Matt said.

Quickly letting go, Jamie stood up as if he'd touched a hot coal. "Whoops," he said, his face going slack. "I'll go tell Dad you're here." He spun on his heels and ran through the kitchen doorway. The thumping of his stockinged feet on the kitchen tile faded and disappeared when he hit the carpet of the dining room.

"Jamie's a little flustered," Judy said.

They walked arm in arm through the kitchen. Matt noticed dishes stacked on the counter. A covered pot on the stove gurgled. The aroma of garlic and spaghetti sauce spiced the air.

Matt's headache intensified as they walked through the brightly lit dining room and into the living room. His head felt like a leaky balloon being blown up by an enthusiastic three-year-old.

Matt looked up and saw Jamie's father, Scott, walking down the stairs. Jamie was right behind him. Scott stopped when he saw Matt and Judy. Scott's smile was reserved, and his eyes looked troubled. Scott had a thin face that sometimes looked very old to Matt and other times almost as young as a boy's. "Hi, Matt. Jamie and I were just making up his bed for you. First time it's been made in a week or so, right, sport?" He shot Jamie a wink and looked back at Matt.

"Are you hungry?" Scott asked, continuing down the stairs. "We've got plenty of dinner waiting."

Matt shook his head no. Moving his head made him dizzy. He leaned on Judy to keep his balance.

"I think we'd better get him up to bed, Scott," Judy said. She sounded tired and impatient.

"Let's sit down and talk for a minute first," Scott said.

"No," Judy said firmly. "Matt should sleep. He needs to rest." She looked up at Scott. "And so do I." Tears welled up in her eyes. Impatiently she brushed them away.

Matt stared at them dumbly. Everyone and everything seemed unreal. Everyone's smile seemed fake. Everyone's long face and movements seemed exaggerated. Everyone's voice was either too loud or too soft. Matt couldn't believe this was happening to him. It seemed like a bad dream. He stared at Jamie and Scott.

"All right, let's get you upstairs and in bed," said Scott. With Judy on one side and Scott on the other, they slowly climbed the stairs, looking like a sorry trio of wounded soldiers.

Jamie was frantically stuffing clothes into dresser drawers when they walked into his room. Clothes were still piled on top of his desk and plopped in most of the nooks and crannies of the room. A few shirts and a pair of jeans on the floor stuck out from under the bed, as if frozen in the act of escaping the dustballs, the dark, and the other clothes that were there.

Jamie turned around and smiled. "Things sure are 'picking up' around here," he quipped.

Matt wanted to smile but his thoughts were flat and heavy. Scott and Judy sat him on the edge of the bed.

"You'll be staying here," said Scott, helping Matt out of his shoes and socks. "We'll clean it up a little more tomorrow." He turned around and asked, "Jamie, do you have an extra pair of pajamas that would fit Matt?"

Matt watched as Jamie plunged up to his elbows into the bottom dresser drawer. Judy and Scott began undressing him. They were careful not to move his shoulder or touch his taped arm. Matt never wore pajamas at home, but he was too tired to argue.

"Here are some," said Jamie, holding up a pair of light blue flannel pajamas. "These should fit."

"Good," said his father. "Matt, could you stand up a minute so we can get these pants off you?" Matt felt silly, having other people unbutton and unzip his jeans. They fell to the floor.

"Let's get these off too," Scott said, pulling down his underwear. Like a robot, Matt stepped out of his pants and underwear and into the pajama bottoms that Jamie held out for him. That accomplished, he sat down heavily, as if he had bricks in the seat of the pajamas.

"Maybe we should forget the top," Judy said. "We shouldn't button it and I don't think it'll stay on anyway."

Scott drew back the covers and helped Matt lie down on his back. He gently pulled the blankets up to Matt's chin and stood up. "Let us know if we can do anything for you tonight, Matt," he said.

Matt nodded. Where will Jamie sleep? he wondered dully. As if she read his mind, Judy bent down to tuck the covers around his chin. "Jamie will be downstairs on the living room sofa camping out," she said.

Judy turned from the bed and pulled the curtain closed. "Goodnight," she said. She took Scott's hand in hers and together they left. Matt and Jamie listened to their quiet voices as they walked down the hall.

Twice Jamie opened his mouth to say something and twice he just gulped air and closed it. On the third try he blurted, "Matt, I'm real sorry." He turned away and grabbed a pile of clothes on the top of his dresser. "I'll need these for school tomorrow." He glanced at Matt, bolted for the door, and just before he flicked off the light he turned and, a hint of tears in his eyes and voice, he said, "Goodnight, Matt."

Matt watched the light from the hall as it was squeezed thin by the door and finally disappeared. Lying down in the dark quiet, Matt's head throbbed less.

Although he had slept in Jamie's room many times, he couldn't quite recognize the objects around him. The room seemed strange, the bed seemed strange, and the house was making little creaking and burping noises followed by strange little smells. The dark and quiet made Matt feel abandoned — overwhelmed by loneliness. His arm began to throb a bit and he shifted his weight, arranging the pillow under his shoulder in a more comfortable position.

And he felt funny wearing pajama bottoms. At home he always slept naked. Matt reached down with his right hand and unsnapped the top of the pajama bottoms. Slowly, mechanically, he slid them down his legs and then pushed them off with his feet. He stuffed them over the edge of the mattress, between the covers and the bed. The sheets felt good against the length of his body.

In the dark, his thoughts seemed louder. Images bumping and tumbling into images, chasing each other slowly at first and then faster and faster until they were racing frantically around his head: his mother turning to talk to him while she was driving, the frantic screams, shattering glass, the crunch of metal, the blinking lights, the drunk man.

Matt tensed. He could see the man in front of him. "You son of a bitch," he hissed at the vision. He tried to think of something worse to say. "You Goddamn son of a bitch." Even that wasn't horrible enough. Words failed him. He wanted to tear the man's eyes out and strangle him.

Matt reached out into the dark toward the man's blubbering face and suddenly he saw the smiling face of his mother.

Startled, he drew back his hand. His mother's face grew clearer, and a halo of light surrounded her head, shimmering through her hair. She seemed so real that Matt could almost smell the perfume she normally wore. Matt stared into her eyes. He followed the line of her nose with his eyes, moving down her face. He saw that her lips were moving silently. They seemed to say, "I love you, Matt. I love you."

A chill spread through his body, followed by a wave of goose bumps. He felt the hair on the back of his head prickle and stand up. Slowly his mother's face faded into the darkness and he was alone.

Horrified, he was struck by the impact of the accident as if he'd been slapped in the face. His mother was dead. She was dead, dead, dead!

Sorrow, fear, love, hate, loneliness — all of these emotions exploded inside of him and a huge, aching wave began in his gut and rolled upward, sucking air into his lungs until they felt like bursting. The agony of this grief doubled Matt up and he clutched his stomach and rolled onto his side. A guttural cry ripped through his throat and exploded into the pillow. Wave after wave of pain and sorrow racked his body, tears washed over his face, and spit dribbled out of the corners of his mouth. Matt gasped for air, unable to control the crying.

35

Quickly the door to his room opened and he felt himself being lifted and cradled in strong arms. "I'm here, Matt. I'm here." He heard Scott's soothing voice close above his head. Scott's breath smelled strongly of spaghetti sauce. Matt cried even harder. His insides felt like they were being yanked apart. He was overwhelmed by the kindness — and he was possessed by grief. His mother was... dead!

Matt cried long and hard. Scott rocked him back and forth and held him close, stroking Matt's head. Tears quietly fell from his own chin onto Matt's shoulder. "I'm here, Matt," he said softly, over and over again.

Slowly the ache in Matt's gut lessened and his sobs became weaker. Matt no longer gasped for air. He gradually relaxed, tired and spent.

Scott held him a while longer and, when Matt's breathing was regular and deep, he carefully laid Matt on the bed. Scott reached down into the covers and fished around for the pajama bottoms. He pulled them out and draped them over the headboard. Tucking the covers under Matt's chin, Scott brushed back the hair stuck to Matt's sweaty forehead.

Scott turned and saw Judy, standing in the doorway. He walked up and hugged her. "He's all right now," he whispered. Scott turned and closed the door quietly with his other hand.

Matt slept soundly. Once during the night he dreamed he saw his sister, face down on the hood of the car, blood dripping into the snow. She began to burble like a distant motorboat. Her arms began to move, making a swimming motion, and she slowly, painfully pulled herself along the length of the hood. As her body emerged from the jagged black hole in the windshield, Matt saw, to his horror, that she had no legs. A trail of blood followed her like the slime of a slug.

His body tensed and his eyes flew open. The nightmare faded slowly, and merciful sleep returned.

Five

alf asleep, his eyes puffy and closed, Matt felt sunlight bathing his face in heat. He opened his eyes slowly, straight into a bright beam of sunlight coming through a slit in the curtains — aimed right at him. It cut through the dimness of the room like a flattened laser beam. Specks of dust floated into it and then scurried out.

His thoughts were muddled by lingering sleep. He felt emotionally bruised and battered — in a fog. The accident. He remembered the accident. The piercing light vaporized the fog in his head, and scenes of the accident blazed across his brain. Matt closed his eyes and the scenes faded.

His eyes were tender. He opened them and squinted about him. Jamie's room looked more picked up than last night. The piles of clothes had disappeared. Looking over his toes, Matt saw that Jamie's desk top was completely clear.

A shiver scurried up and then down his spine and Matt reached down with his good arm and pulled up the covers that lay swirled at his feet.

He scrunched his eyes tighter and looked through his

eyelashes at the light coming from the curtains. It was too strong and bright for early morning. I wonder what time it is, he thought.

The beam fell on the wall opposite the window, making a stripe down the door of Jamie's closet. Matt pictured, under the shoes piled in the back closet corner, the dirty magazines and the old pack of stale cigarettes he and Jamie had hidden there. Occasionally he and Jamie found treasures like this in a secluded picnic area near the Fletcher house. High school kids and college students sometimes camped there or had parties. They always left lots of trash, mostly empty beer, wine, and liquor bottles. Sometimes he and Jamie found dirty magazines and shirts and socks and other loot.

Whenever Matt or Jamie found interesting booty they sneaked it into the back of Jamie's closet — "So the little kids don't find it," Jamie always said, laughing.

Matt could never keep things like that at his house because his mother constantly cleaned up his room, including his closets. He pictured his mother, her rear end sticking out of his closet, as she lined up his shoes or pulled out the dirty socks he always stuffed in them. Matt's throat tightened and his eyes filled with tears. He blinked several times and swallowed hard. The tears went away, but the aching deep inside remained.

Secret places. Matt looked up at the books on the top shelf above Jamie's desk. At the right end a thick volume, a Reader's Digest Condensed Book, separated the dictionary from the books on airplanes that Jamie was fond of. With his pocket knife, Jamie had carved out a square hole in the middle of each page of this book — from 50 to 300.

Unopened, the book looked perfectly normal. And the hollow inside was perfect for hiding paper money and notes.

"That book is really condensed now," Jamie had said when he showed it to Matt. "A 'hole' lot." To prove to Jamie that he'd never tell anyone about the secret money book, Matt matched the five-dollar bill Jamie hid inside with one of his own. They recorded the amount on the bottom of page 100, the amount of money each of them wanted to save by the end of the year.

Matt lay back, looked at the ceiling, and closed his eyes. He tried not to think of his mother or Jeannie or the accident. He tried not to think about what would have happened to him if, instead of Jeannie, he'd been in the front seat. Matt concentrated on the faint jabber of a radio downstairs. He breathed deeply. The room smelled stale. The furnace blew hot air out of a vent on the floor to the right of the bed every couple of seconds. House farts, Matt thought.

Matt had almost dozed off when he heard steps coming down the hall. He heard the door open and his nose tingled with the smell of toast and eggs and bacon.

Sleepily, he forced his eyes open, expecting to see his mother. Instead he saw Judy standing in the doorway carrying a breakfast tray. She looked tired, but she was smiling.

"Good morning, Matt," she said, taking a deep breath. She set the tray down on Jamie's desk. "You sure slept late this morning!" Judy walked over to the window and pulled the curtains open. Light burst in and Matt blinked as his eyes watered.

"Hi," he said, struggling to sit up. His voice sounded like a frog. "What time is it?" he croaked.

"About nine." Judy walked over to the bed. "Jamie wanted to wake you up before he went to school. He had a joke he wanted to tell you." Her mouth was smiling but her eyes were not. "That Jamie. Always joking — just like his father," she said. "How do you feel?" She bent down and put a hand on his forehead.

"Sleepy," Matt said. "And my head still hurts a little."

"Well, Dr. Woods told me to keep you in bed and to keep you quiet," Judy said, standing up and turning toward Jamie's desk. "You don't have a fever, but I bet you're starved." She picked up the tray. "You haven't had much to eat since the..." She stopped and her mouth opened and closed like a startled guppy's. Taking a deep breath she continued, "... since the day before yesterday. I fixed you a big breakfast, but you don't have to eat it all."

Matt looked at the breakfast. Steam rose from the scrambled eggs and a lump of butter was disappearing into the toast. Next to the eggs were three strips of bacon.

Matt stared at the bacon. His mother never let him eat bacon or sausage or hot dogs. She called them "trash" meats. But Matt loved them. He thought of the times he and Jamie sneaked hot dogs out of the Fletcher refrigerator and ate them cold. When he was little, Matt sometimes dreamed about hot dogs and how good they tasted, even though they almost always gave him a stomachache. He wanted to taste the bacon, but he felt guilty even thinking about it. He took a sip of juice.

"We have a lot of things to talk about, Matt," Judy said, sitting down at the foot of the bed. "I want you to let me know about things you like to eat. We've known you since you were born," she added. "But we have so many things to learn about each other."

Matt took a bite of eggs. His tongue felt thick and numb. He could hardly taste the eggs at all. His throat was tight, almost raw, and swallowing took concentration.

Judy stood up. "I'll be back in a second."

Matt continued to eat. The food sat in his stomach like a pouting toad. Almost every bite, bits of scrambled eggs tumbled off his fork and into his lap before he reached his mouth. The more he tried to steady the fork, the more his hand shook. He grabbed the fork with both hands and lifted it as high up as he could before his left arm began to hurt. At that point, he bent down and stretched his neck to meet the food halfway.

Matt's mind wandered as he ate. Into his mind popped his first memory of Judy. One day, when he was very small, he asked his mother for some ice cream. She had told him to wait for dinner. But Matt wanted ice cream and wasn't going to take "no" for an answer. He walked up the street to Jamie's house. He marched up the front steps, reached up, and rang the doorbell.

Judy had come to the door, looking surprised to see him. She opened the screen door and said, "It's good to see you, Matt. Do you want to play with Jamie?"

"No," Matt had said. "My mother wants to borrow some ice cream."

Judy looked surprised. "Ice cream?" Matt nodded. "Well, come on in."

She took him to the kitchen and opened up the freezer.

"Chocolate all right?" He nodded. "Does she want the whole container?"

"No," Matt said. "Just a bowl."

Judy dug up a bowl full and handed it to Matt.

"She wants chocolate on it, too," he said.

Judy got some chocolate syrup from the refrigerator and poured some onto the ice cream. "Would she like a spoon?" Judy asked.

"Yes, please," Matt said.

Judy stuck a spoon in the ice cream and walked Matt to the door.

"Say hi to your mom for me," she said as he walked down the stairs, balancing the ice cream. His mouth was watering. "And tell her I have more ice cream if she wants it."

Matt ate the ice cream before he got home and put the bowl and spoon on the kitchen table when he walked in. "Judy says hi," he told his mother, who looked in surprise at the bowl and spoon.

His mother figured it out right away. She called Judy and they laughed and laughed on the phone. She tried to scold Matt, but she couldn't stop smiling. She gave up and sent Matt back with the washed bowl and spoon. For a long time after that, whenever Matt came calling, Judy asked him if his mother wanted some ice cream. Then she almost always chuckled. Matt never understood what was so funny. And Judy laughed out loud when he said, "Yes."

Matt wrestled with the last scrap of egg when Judy walked into the room, carrying a note card. "All done?" she asked.

Matt nodded his head. "Thanks," he said. His voice was still raw. Judy took the tray and put it on Jamie's desk. She sat on the bed facing him. She put a note card on her lap and took his right hand in both of hers.

"Matt, I have a couple of errands to run," she said. "First, I'm going to meet with Scott and talk to some people about your mother's will." She paused and took a deep breath. "And I'm going to talk to some people about your mother's funeral. She'll be buried on Thursday."

Matt pictured the spot in the cemetery where his father was buried. It was a quiet corner, near a field of coal-black soil normally planted in corn. Marking the grave was a low, reddish stone, flat and polished on top. His father's name was carved in plain letters on the left: Matthew R. Smythe. That was Matt's name, too, even though his mother used it only when he was in trouble.

Matt hated to go to the cemetery. This dislike always upset his mother, but he never told her why. Matt hated to look at the name he shared with his father. A cemetery was a place for dead people's names, not live people's. And he always felt he was looking at his own name.

There was one difference, though. Below his father's name was carved the year in which he was born and the year in which he died — separated by a short dash that Matt used to think meant his father's life had been short.

On the other half of the stone was his mother's name. Matt always felt creepy looking at his mother's name. Underneath her name was the year in which she was born, a dash and a blank space.

On one of their few trips to the cemetery, Matt asked

his mother why her name was on the stone. "You're not dead and buried," he said pointedly.

"No," she replied. "But when I am, this is where I'll be, right next to your father."

Somehow, to Matt, there never looked like enough room for both of them, side by side, beneath that stone.

His thoughts were interrupted by Judy's voice. "These are some numbers you can call if you need anything while I'm gone," she said. "This first one is Scott's. His secretary will know how to get hold of us. And here is the number of Mrs. Sanger, next door."

Great, Matt thought. "Old Witch" Sanger. Last year she'd caught him, with Jamie and some of their friends, behind the Fletcher house stuffing firecrackers into anthills and blowing them up. She'd scolded them in her shrill voice and, that evening, she'd called every one of their parents.

"Do you think you'll be OK?" Judy asked.

Matt nodded. "Yes," he said. "Thanks for the breakfast." How many times did I thank Mom for breakfast? he wondered. He couldn't think of a single time. He felt sad.

Judy smiled and stood up. She put the notecard on Jamie's desk and picked up the breakfast tray. "I hope I'm not gone long," she said. "Oh, I almost forgot. I may be going to your house to pick up some clothes for you. Do you want anything else?"

Matt thought for a moment. "My pillow," he said. His pillow was filled with down, which he could pound into any shape he wanted. He always slept better with it than any other pillow. "And my toothbrush," he said, feeling his fuzzy teeth with the tip of his tongue.

"OK," Judy said. Still holding the tray, she bent down and kissed him on the forehead. "Would you like the door open?" Matt nodded yes.

Matt listened as Judy rummaged around downstairs. The kitchen door slammed, the car started, and Matt could hear it going down the driveway and, with a muffled roar, down the street.

He sat up carefully, took a deep breath, and pushed himself to his feet with his good arm. So far so good. He felt weak and a little dizzy — but not too bad. He shuffled to the window and looked out.

The snow was bright, covering bushes and trees in heavy globs. As he watched, a glob on a nearby branch slid off and plopped onto the snow below. The branch, free of the snow's weight, snapped back, sending shivers to nearby branches. Several other branches shed their snow until, finally, the chain reaction stopped and the tree was still. Underneath, surrounding the trunk, were pocks in the snow, looking like craters on the face of the moon.

Even though he was alone in the house, Matt reached for the pajama bottoms draped on the headboard and put them on. He walked slowly down the hall to the bathroom.

Relieved, feeling much better, Matt slowly made his way back to Jamie's bedroom. He took off the pajamas and crawled under the covers.

Although his head didn't hurt as much as the evening before, Matt felt light-headed. He was completely tuckered out after his walk to the bathroom.

Matt lay in bed, listening to his heart beating. Without thinking he reached toward his crotch and felt himself as he sometimes did when he was lonely or sad. He felt oddly small and cold. A warm feeling grew as he touched himself. It felt good.

Matt closed his eyes as he fondled himself. Suddenly a vivid picture of the accident — and the faces of his mother and sister — flashed across his mind. His hand froze where it was.

Matt's mind was alive with thoughts, thoughts flopping around in his head. If my mother is dead, Matt thought frantically, she must be in heaven. If she's in heaven she must be looking down at me. If she's looking down at me, she must see what I'm doing to myself.

Breathlessly, these thoughts repeated themselves over and over. He drew his hand from his crotch and held it against the sling.

Can she see me? Matt was horrified. *Or worse, can she hear my thoughts?*

Six

he morning dragged, moving as fast as a tree growing. Matt tried not to think about the accident, but it was hard. Images sneaked up on him and held his thoughts hostage unless he fought them off. To make the time go faster and keep his mind off sad thoughts, Matt lay in bed for a while closing his eyes and opening them when he thought five minutes had gone by. The first time he opened his eyes and checked Jamie's alarm clock, only two minutes had passed. The next time he scrunched his eyes together. When he thought five minutes were up, he held his breath, and when he couldn't stand it any longer he opened his eyes and looked. Three minutes. It had seemed like thirty!

Matt quickly tired of this game. To keep himself occupied, he decided to dress before Judy got home. With only one arm it took all of his concentration. He borrowed a clean pair of Jamie's underwear and got it on only to find it was on backward. The jeans were a lot tougher. The button didn't want to button without the zipper being zipped. And the zipper didn't want to zip up without the button being buttoned.

48

Just as he finally got himself buttoned and zipped, the telephone rang. Matt jumped and scurried for the phone in Judy's and Scott's bedroom.

"Hello," Matt said breathlessly. Nobody said anything at the other end. But Matt thought he heard a sniffle. "Hello?" Matt heard a click followed by the dial tone.

Must have been a wrong number, Matt thought. But just as he reached the bedroom door, it rang again. Matt rushed back and pounced on the phone, right in the middle of a ring. "Hello," he said, a little annoyed. Somebody coughed at the other end.

"Ah . . ." The person coughed again. "Can I speak to Matt?"

Matt was taken aback. He didn't expect the caller to want him. This wasn't his home! "I'm Matt," he said, haltingly. *Who is this, anyway?*

"Matt, I'm Ralph."

Ralph. It was! Jeannie's boyfriend, Ralph. "Hi, Ralph," Matt said.

"How are you?" Ralph asked.

"Fine."

"You sound OK," Ralph said.

"Thanks." This sure is a weird conversation, Matt thought.

"Matt, how's Jeannie?" Ralph sounded on the verge of crying.

"She's hurt pretty bad," Matt said. Whatever that means, he thought. Suddenly the conversation made sense.

"How bad?" Ralph asked.

"I don't know," Matt said.

"Oh." Ralph paused. "Maybe I'll call back later. Matt?"

"Ya?"

49

"I feel terrible about everything. I...I..." and Ralph hung up.

Matt's head began to pound a little. I better lie down, he thought. He walked back to Jamie's room.

As he lay down, Matt thought about Ralph and Jeannie. They had been going together since they were seven or eight. If they ever "tied the knot," their mother joked, it would be a square knot. Jeannie usually blushed and told her mother that it would be a "slipknot or not at all."

Matt was dozing off when he heard the kitchen door slam and Judy's voice. "I'm home," she yelled.

Judy pounded up the stairs and breathlessly swooped into the room, clothes draped over her shoulders and arms. In one hand she held a hanger, laden with his sports jacket, button-down shirt, tie, and dress pants. In the other hand she held his penny loafers.

"I brought these for you, Matt," she said, laying the loaded hanger and other clothes at the foot of the bed.

Matt looked at them — his favorite T-shirt, some polo shirts, another pair of jeans, some underwear, and some socks. Those were all right.

"Why did you bring these?" he asked, pointing to the dress clothes. He didn't like wearing them. They reminded him of church.

"I thought you could wear these on Thursday," she said. "For your mother's funeral." Judy began picking up the clothes. "If you don't like them, we can get more clothes tomorrow after we visit the doctor," she said.

"Thanks," Matt said, looking up and faking a smile.

"And I talked to your mother's minister," Judy said. "He wants to come over and talk with you this afternoon."

Matt pictured the minister at the church they sometimes went to. His last name was Untterbach. The preacher had a face that always reminded Matt of a potato. Its shape was irregular and his eyes were uneven. His mouth looked like the gash of a careless paring knife. When Mr. Untterbach talked, his cheeks developed lumps that made him look like he was talking with his mouth full of tough steak.

Another thing always struck Matt. The preacher's voice sounded like mashed potatoes felt — thick and mushy.

The Reverend Mr. Untterbach carried himself with great dignity, which wasn't always easy. Matt remembered one of his sermons. The preacher was yelling and waving his arms and dripping sweat onto his text. Suddenly, in the middle of a word, when he was bellowing his loudest, he sneezed. The sneeze woke a few people up, including a choir member, who sat bolt upright, blurting, "God bless you!"

A few people in the congregation began to snicker and, as Mr. Untterbach took out his hankie and began to wipe his nose and mouth, a few more began to laugh. Soon whole pews were shaking.

Matt pinched the inside of his wrist to keep from laughing. The preacher put his hankie away and looked down at his text. Matt noticed that the minister's blushing scalp shone through his whitish blond hair, making it orange, like a fuzzy carrot. Mr. Untterbach looked up, smiled vaguely, and said, "I guess I got edited by the Author Himself."

The congregation roared. Matt had never heard laughter in a sanctuary before. It sounded nice.

51

Mr. Untterbach signaled the organist to begin the next hymn, and the laughter turned to singing.

"Oh, I almost forgot," Judy said, putting the last of Matt's clothes in a dresser drawer. "Your pillow."

She rushed out of the room and down the stairs. Almost as quickly, she was back, holding the pillow and breathing hard. "I'll . . . go . . . downstairs . . . and . . . weave for a while," she managed to say. "Call if you . . . need anything."

For as long as Matt could remember, Judy had woven rugs and blankets on a loom that filled up almost half of the downstairs study. Matt's mother thought Judy's weavings were beautiful. So did Matt. But Judy was never satisfied. "When I can weave something as beautiful as a spiderweb I'll really have something," she once told Matt.

Matt could watch knitting fingers for hours. Watching Judy at her loom affected him in the same way. When Judy really got going, her feet moving and her fingers dancing over the strings of the warp like a harpist's fingers over the strings of a harp, Matt was mesmerized. He listened carefully for the soft bumping rhythm of the loom. As Judy warmed up to her weaving, the bump-bump became more regular and more lively. Matt tried to think of something else that made such a sound. A tennis ball bouncing off a backboard and onto the court came close, but not quite close enough.

Matt felt the need to keep busy, to keep his mind occupied. He got up and snooped around Jamie's room. He counted the money in Jamie's money book twice — coming up with $27. Matt was sitting up in Jamie's bed, ready to count the money a third time, when Judy walked in carrying a tray with lunch. Matt quickly stuffed the money book under his pillow and pretended to fluff it up.

"A little sandwich and juice," Judy said, handing Matt the tray.

Matt looked at the food. "Thanks," he said. He looked at Judy's face, her forehead wrinkled slightly in concern. He smiled and her face relaxed.

"Well, I better get busy. Just put the tray on the desk when you're finished." Judy turned toward the door. "By the way," she said over her shoulder, "don't tell Jamie, but I owe him five dollars. Reader's Digest didn't exactly make me a sweepstakes winner, but . . ." She walked out of the room.

Matt's jaw dropped. "I wonder what else she knows about," he muttered.

After eating, Matt prowled the room some more. He flipped through some of Jamie's books. Jamie had a thing about books. He wouldn't read one for fun unless he owned it. And he kept them arranged alphabetically by author. Smiling, Matt took a "T" book and put it with the "M" books.

His eyelids began to droop and he was nodding off when he heard the kitchen door slam and Jamie's voice yelling hello to his mother. Footsteps pounded up the stairs and Jamie burst into the room, still taking off his parka.

He skidded to a stop, looked at Matt, and suddenly his eyes grew shy. "Hi, Matt," he said, breathing heavily and plopping his parka on the floor by the desk.

"Hi," Matt said.

"Whatcha up to?" Jamie asked, moving closer to the bed and cramming his hands into his pockets.

53

"Less than seven feet but more than four," Matt said.

Jamie's face split into a grin. "Yep, there's Matt: the world's smallest giant. Or," he chuckled, "the world's tallest midget."

"How was school?" Matt asked.

"Pretty boring," Jamie answered, sitting on the foot of the bed. "Except that Melanie stayed in the bathroom almost a half an hour during math, and Mr. Roberts went in and dragged her out."

Mr. Roberts was their math and homeroom teacher. And Melanie was always in the bathroom goofing off. She thought that a man teacher would never walk into the girls' restroom to get her.

"She must have been real embarrassed," Matt said.

"Ya," Jamie agreed. "I think she was 'em-bare-assed.'" He wiggled his hips, making the bed bounce. Matt smiled.

They heard a car drive into the driveway, and a car door slammed shut. Jamie walked over to the window, his hands still in his pockets, and looked out.

"Mr. Untterbach," he whispered, turning toward Matt. He looked worried. "I-I think I'll go see if I can help Mom with supper." And he scurried off.

Matt heard voices downstairs, one of them low and mushy. It sounded like Mr. Untterbach. The voices grew louder.

"We were such good friends," he heard Judy saying. "It just hasn't sunk in yet." She paused. "But I just can't let myself fall apart while Matt needs me. None of us can."

"It's a selfless thing you're doing," the preacher said, "not giving in to your own grief. If you need any help..."

Judy was ushered awkwardly into the room by the preacher, who then stepped in behind her and smiled at

Matt. His face looked lumpier than usual. "Good afternoon, Matt," he said. He turned to Judy. "Could we be alone?"

"Of course," Judy answered. She looked relieved as she turned and closed the door behind her.

Mr. Untterbach pulled Jamie's desk chair by the bed and sat down. With a flourish, he draped one leg over the other and cupped the top knee in both of his hands. His hands were big. And his thin smile never faded.

"We were all saddened when we heard of your mother's death," he began. He sounded like his tongue was too big for his mouth. "She was a wonderful, strong woman who overcame so much to bring you and your sister up right."

Matt looked at the preacher. The tangy smell of after-shave mingled with bad coffee breath.

"And now, you must be as strong as your mother to overcome this tragedy," he continued. His gaze never faltered. "Judy says that you've been very quiet and withdrawn since the accident. That's only natural. It has been a terrible shock to us all, especially you, and we want to help."

Matt looked down at his own feet. Since the preacher had been talking, one question had been gathering, like a dark cloud, in his mind. He took a deep breath.

"Why did my mother die?" he asked, looking up. The loudness of his voice, and the anger in it, surprised Matt himself.

The preacher gazed out the window a moment and then, turning his head toward Matt, he said, "I don't know why your mother died. Nobody but the Lord knows. But the Lord has His reasons. We must trust Him and know that He is good."

Matt could feel anger bubbling up. "How could God kill somebody?" he demanded. "How could God let some . . . some drunk crash into us and kill my mother?" Tears welled up in his eyes, and his throat tightened. He suddenly wished he knew more swear words.

"Now, now, Matt," Mr. Untterbach said, putting both feet on the floor and leaning forward. His eyes were looking above Matt's head. Matt sat up straighter so their eyes would meet. The preacher's eyes looked wary, uncomfortable. "The Lord didn't kill your mother," he said.

"If He's so big and powerful and good, then why didn't He stop that drunk man from killing her?" Matt's voice grew louder with every word and was climbing in pitch.

"Matt, the Lord works in mysterious ways. We don't always understand why He does what He does or why He lets some things happen. But Matt, your mother is in heaven . . . with Him. He must have wanted her closer to Him."

"*I* want my mother!" Matt yelled. "*I* want her! She's *my* mother and He's selfish and . . . and horrible and . . . and nasty and *mean* to take her!"

"Matt," Mr. Untterbach said, reaching out to take Matt's hand. Matt yanked it away and drew his knees up to his chest. Matt was furious — with this man, with God, with everything. The preacher was not put off. "Try to understand," he said. "We are all children of the Lord and He looks after us, even when we don't have parents to look after us."

Matt seethed. He glared at the preacher. His jaw was set, jutting.

Mr. Untterbach looked at Matt sadly. "Matt," he said,

bowing his head and clasping his hands together. "Let's pray. 'Our Father, who art . . .' "

Matt tuned him out and looked at the whitish blond hair on the top of Mr. Untterbach's bowed head. *I wish he'd go away. My mother is dead. And this man is trying to tell me it's OK! He's trying to tell me it's all right!*

Matt began to tremble. His head began to pound. His eyes dripped tears. This man was trying to lie to him — tell him things that weren't true! I don't believe in God anyway, Matt thought. But if I ever meet Him I'll slug Him in his Goddamned face!

" '. . . for thine is the Kingdom and the power and the glory forever and ever. Amen.' " Mr. Untterbach's voice trailed off and he looked up at Matt.

"Matt, I know it hurts and I know it's hard to understand. But put your trust in the Lord. He'll help you through this bad time."

The preacher stood up to go. "Judy and Scott are fine people. Let them help. And I'll help as much as I can." Quietly he turned and left. The door clicked shut behind him like a gun that hadn't gone off.

Matt's head exploded with pent-up anger. He couldn't believe what had just happened. His trembling got worse. His breathing became labored, as if the preacher had taken half the air with him when he left. An uncontrollable rage possessed him.

"Bullshit!" Matt fumed through clenched teeth. "God-damn Him to hell — and that drunk too! I hate Him! I hate them both!" Matt's voice burned and the veins on either side of his neck felt like they would burst. Matt grabbed an edge of his pillow with his good arm. He sat up and yanked it off the bed.

Matt scrambled off the bed, dropped to his knees, and pounded the floor with the pillow. He drew back and pictured the preacher's face where the pillow hit. "Bullshit! Bullshit! Bullshit!" Matt was hysterical. He struck again and again with the pillow. He scrambled to his feet and kicked at the pillow.

Suddenly, remembering the money book that had been under the pillow, Matt reached around and grabbed it. In a rage, Matt hurled the book at the door.

"GODDAMN YOU!" Matt screeched. Tears poured down his face and into his contorted mouth. He crumpled onto the floor, sobbing, and buried his face in the pillow. He heard the door open and lifted his head, expecting to see Mr. Untterbach. Instead, through his tears, he saw Jamie's horrified face.

"Are you all right?" Jamie asked in a shaky voice. He looked at the floor by the door and saw the money book and money scattered around. His eyes opened wider.

Matt looked at his friend's hurt face and collapsed into his pillow, crying harder.

Matt cried himself out and, feeling miserable and stuffed up, he went to the bathroom to clean up. Jamie had left as soon as he'd picked up his money and money book.

Trying to wash his face with one hand was difficult, especially because he couldn't cup his hands to rinse off the soap. He slipped his arm out of the sling.

Matt's shoulder was sore and his elbow was stiff. His joints popped a little as he extended his arm. Even though the arm and shoulder felt better than he expected, almost normal, Matt put the sling back on when he finished.

Before dinner the air in the house seemed prickly with static electricity, like the air before a thunderstorm. Judy looked worn and tired, but Scott tried to liven everybody up at dinner. They were having pork chops.

"Pass the dead pig," Scott said to Judy, as they sat down.

"Scott, that's enough of that," Judy said.

"OK, pass me the premasticated tubers."

"The what?" Jamie asked.

"Mashed potatoes, you bipedal carnivore," Scott said.

"Really," said Judy. "You're teaching these kids bad manners, Scott."

"Bad manners?" he asked, with a twinkle in his eyes. "I'm teaching them honesty. This," he said, taking a pork chop, "is dead pig—I hope it's dead." He shook it on the fork. "That," he said, pointing to the potatoes, "are premasticated tubers. Should I teach them to be dishonest?"

"No," Judy said. "But when honesty takes away my appetite, we don't need it at the table."

"OK, OK," Scott said. He sounded disappointed that nobody laughed at his joke. "I was only 'porking' fun."

That night, as he was tucking Matt into bed, Scott leaned over to Matt and whispered in his ear. "Don't let Untterbach get to you, Matt. Let your feelings out. We love you no matter what." Scott rumpled Matt's hair and stood up.

"Scott?"

"Yes, Matt?"

"What will happen to the guy who killed my mother?"

Scott sat down on the edge of the bed. "Mr. Porter?

He'll be charged with involuntary manslaughter," he said. "He's an alcoholic, though, Matt, and I don't know what will happen to him."

"Will they put him in jail?"

"I don't know," Scott said.

"Will they put him in the gas chamber?"

"I don't think so. Do you want him to die?"

"He's a son of a bitch!" Matt hissed.

Scott nodded his head. He looked sad and tired. "Keep me posted on what you're feeling, Matt," he said, patting Matt's knee. "I'll keep you posted on Mr. Porter. Deal?"

Matt nodded. With a grunt Scott got up. "Got to get these old bones to bed. Goodnight, Matt." He turned out the light and closed the door.

Thoughts of the dinner conversation kept bubbling up, like burps. The conversation — and the dinner, for that matter — had been unsettling.

Dead pig. We eat dead things to stay alive. Death becomes life. Matt shook his head to get rid of these thoughts. He tried to think of pleasant things — rainbows, roses, fresh-cut grass. But he still couldn't get rid of the taste of pork chops in his mouth or the thoughts of dead pig.

He finally slept. But his dreams were crowded with morbid thoughts. In one he heard a deep, booming voice say, "Pass the dead mother, please."

"Death becomes life up here, you know," another booming voice said. "Love these dead mothers. Pass the salt?"

Matt started awake, shaking, in a cold sweat. It was too horrible to think about, and it took a long time before he fell back asleep.

Seven

G roggy *with sleep, Matt heard little scritching* noises — like mice running up and down the dresser top. Slowly, he opened one eye.

Just as he suspected. Instead of mice he saw Jamie rummaging around in his dresser, looking for clothes. Jamie was still in his pajamas.

I'll surprise him, Matt thought. Layers of sleep peeled away and he mentally readied himself. With a whispered "Roar" he sat up and tried to pounce at the same time. Matt forgot, though, that his right arm was held in the sling. Instead of going forward, he flopped backward onto the bed.

Jamie jumped in surprise and spun around. When he saw Matt struggling to get untangled from the covers, Jamie laughed.

"Gotcha!" he said, jumping on top of Matt and sitting on his stomach.

"I almost had you," Matt said, trying to wriggle out from under Jamie.

"But I've got you!" Jamie beamed. Jamie wasn't often

on top in wrestling matches. He began tickling Matt, who thrashed with his feet and laughed uncontrollably.

"No fair!" Matt gasped. "I've only got one arm!"

"And I've only got one head, so there!" Jamie jumped off the bed and stood by the dresser grinning at Matt, out of breath. "Why don't you get some clothes on, you nudist," he said.

Matt looked down. Sure enough, during the night he'd managed to wriggle out of the pajama bottoms. He grabbed some covers and pulled them up. "What time is it, anyway?" he asked.

"About seven," Jamie answered. "I came in to get some clothes for school. We have gym today." Jamie turned back to the dressers and, with a triumphant "aha!" pulled out a shirt. "I knew it was in there," he said.

Jamie gathered the clothes on the top of the dresser together and plopped them at the foot of the bed. He took off his pajamas and started to get dressed.

"When do you think you'll go back to school, Matt?" Jamie asked, buttoning up his shirt. Matt thought it was odd that Jamie didn't put on his underwear first.

"I guess we go to the doctor today," Matt replied. "He'll tell me. But I feel fine."

"Mr. Roberts told our homeroom he didn't think you'd be back for a while." Jamie looked up at Matt, as if he'd said something he shouldn't have. Embarrassed, he reached for his underwear. "But yesterday he asked me to have a business lunch with him." Matt and Jamie sometimes ate lunch with Mr. Roberts in the homeroom whenever he had something to talk with them about or if they wanted to talk with him about something. Mostly lunch with Mr.

Roberts was just for fun, but he called them business lunches anyway.

"Oh ya? What did you talk about?" Matt asked.

"Well, he wanted to know how you were doing," Jamie answered. "And he wanted to know if you'll be living with us from now on." Jamie reached for his jeans and put them on. He looked straight at Matt while he zipped and buttoned the jeans.

Matt looked back at Jamie, who sat down on the bed and began putting on his socks and shoes. He thought for a moment. Both sets of his grandparents were dead. He had no aunts or uncles — only a great-uncle who lived in Alaska. Matt had never met him before. "Jamie, do you think your parents will ... adopt me?"

"I think they'd like to if it's OK with you," Jamie said, tying his shoes. He put his foot on the floor and looked at Matt. "I guess that would make us brothers, huh?"

Matt stared at Jamie. Jamie was his best friend. He didn't fight with Jamie the way he fought with his sister, or the way most of his friends fought with their brothers and sisters. Brothers and sisters were supposed to be people you would never choose to be friends, but if anybody picked on them you'd stick up for your brother or sister, even if it meant fighting — and getting whipped.

Could best friends be brothers? Or more important, could brothers be best friends?

"I hope you stay," said Jamie. "I've always wanted a brother." He stood up and looked at Matt.

"So have I," Matt said, quietly. A smile crept over his face. "That would make me the older brother," he said.

*   *   *

Brothers. Sisters. After Jamie left, Matt's head filled with thoughts about his sister.

Jeannie loved to read in the window seat upstairs in her bedroom. She would curl up for hours with a book — reading, gazing out the window, and then reading some more. Matt often saw her when he walked up the driveway, propped up by pillows, sitting at the window looking totally absorbed in her knees.

One summer day, Matt remembered, his sister opened the window wide, settled in to read, and promptly fell asleep. She not only fell asleep, she began listing to one side and almost fell out of the window. She caught herself just in time by grabbing the curtains. "I had no choice," she joked nervously after the incident. "It was curtains either way."

Jeannie called her window seat her "window to the world." She loved to daydream and let her mind wander when she read.

"A good writer," she once told Matt, "is like a good artist, only he paints pictures in your mind."

"Does he stick the brush up your nose or in your ears?" Matt asked.

"That's gross," Jeannie said, with a toss of her head. "I should know better than to discuss important things with you."

One spring evening, right after dinner, Matt was in his room trying to figure out long division. Suddenly he heard Jeannie scream next door. He heard her feet hit the floor as she ran across her room and burst into his.

"What's going on?" Matt asked, a little annoyed. Two hundred and sixty-four wasn't going into seven hundred and three very easily. "Did you read something scary?" He looked up and saw that his sister was as white as a sheet.

"No," she said. She was breathing very hard for such a short run. "I was sitting by my window when something *smashed* into it." She looked at Matt, her eyes fluttering. "I think it was a *bird!*" Her eyes grew wide.

Matt got up from his math and followed Jeannie down the stairs. They went outside and circled to the front of the house. The sun was setting and the window glinted with brilliant oranges and yellows. As the colors faded, the light from inside Jeannie's bedroom shone more bravely.

Matt could see a smudgy mark on one of the window panes, as if somebody had thrown a dirty washrag at it.

"It should be behind these bushes," Matt said. He dropped to his knees and worked his way through the bushes. He could see very little in the fading light except leaves and twigs that had fallen from the bushes. He held his breath and listened for movements. To his left he heard a faint rustling followed by an even fainter "cheep."

"I think I found it," he whispered. He slowly inched his way toward the sounds and, looking closely, he saw a bird lying on its side.

He carefully scooped it up in his hands and tried to back out of the bushes. The branches grabbed at him and snagged on his shirt.

"Could you help me get out of here?" he asked impatiently.

Jeannie parted the bushes and Matt scooted out on his knees. "Let me see!" she whispered. The sunlight was too dim, so they walked over to the light streaming from the living room window.

"It's a robin!" Jeannie said. "And it's alive!"

Matt had never held a bird in his hands before and he suddenly felt afraid that it would start fluttering or begin to peck at him.

"Here, you take it," Matt said. Jeannie reluctantly held out her hands and Matt carefully placed the robin in them.

Jeannie stared into her palms, a reverent look on her face. "We better get it inside," she whispered.

They walked around to the back. Matt opened the kitchen door for Jeannie. She pressed her elbows against her sides, to steady her arms, as they slowly walked through the house and to the stairs.

"Would you go upstairs and get the box of tissues in the bathroom?" she asked. "Tear away the top and crumple up some tissues on top of the ones in the box."

Matt ran up to the bathroom, made the tissue box nest, and took it to Jeannie's bedroom. Jeannie was sitting on the edge of her bed, holding the bird in her cupped hands like a soap bubble that would burst if she even thought about moving. Matt put the box on her knees and steadied it as Jeannie carefully placed the bird inside.

They studied the bird, amazed. The feathers were delicately arranged around its head. The beak was like polished stone. And Matt was surprised to see little whiskers sticking out in back of its beak, starting where the upper and lower beaks came together. Little whitish down feathers stuck up between feathers that had been ruffled.

"I think it's still alive," Matt whispered.

"Of course it is, stupid," Jeannie said. "It's breathing."

66

They continued to stare, afraid that the bird would stop breathing in front of their eyes. Matt had never seen anything larger than a worm die before.

"Look!" Matt said. "It's moving!" They watched as the bird opened and closed its mouth several times. Its eyes blinked open and its feet twitched slightly. It made a jerky effort to right itself and flopped back on its side.

"Ooo," Jeannie gasped, tensing. "Ooo!"

"Maybe it broke its wings," Matt said. The bird didn't look very good to him. It was breathing very quickly. Matt tried to breathe in unison with the bird. He couldn't keep up and still get enough air.

"Maybe it cracked its skull," Jeannie said. The bird didn't try to get up again. It just lay on the tissue with its eyes closed.

"Well," Matt said. "I've got some homework to finish. God, I hate mathematics."

Jeannie kept staring at the bird. "It's so beautiful!" she said. "I hope it lives."

Later that night, Matt felt his bed jump. Sleepily he looked up and saw Jeannie sitting next to him, tears pouring down her face and dripping into her lap.

"It's dead!" she said and then she began to sob.

Matt propped himself up on his elbow. "It's dead?" he asked, still in a fog.

"I woke up and . . . and I leaned over to check it and . . . and it was dead!" Jeannie blubbered.

"Are you sure?" Matt asked. He got up and walked with Jeannie to her room.

On the floor, next to Jeannie's nightstand, was the box.

Matt walked over to it, picked it up carefully and held it up to Jeannie's reading lamp. The legs were straight and stiff. The eyes were sunken. Matt poked the bird's chest gently with his finger. It felt hard.

"It's dead," he said, putting the box back on the floor.

"What should we do?" Jeannie asked. Matt hadn't seen her so distressed since the time Ralph forgot to pick her up for a movie date several months before.

"I don't know. I guess we should wait until tomorrow and bury it." Matt was beginning to feel a little chilly standing in her room with nothing on. He wanted to get back to his warm blankets, curl up, and fall asleep.

"But what will we do tonight?" Jeannie asked. "I don't want to sleep with a dead thing in my room!"

Matt stared at his sister. She wasn't joking. She really didn't want the bird in her room now that it was dead.

"OK," he said. "I'll take it to my room." He picked up the box and walked to the door. He turned around. "Goodnight," he said.

Matt put the box on his desk. It's just a dead bird, he thought. But before he crawled into bed, he piled a handful of dirty clothes on top of the box, just in case.

The next day was Saturday. Matt had just turned his back on the brightening window and was just about to fall back into luxurious sleep when he heard a soft knock on his door.

"Ya," he mumbled, not opening his eyes. He felt the air stir as the door opened.

"Matt?" It was Jeannie, dressed in her jeans and a sweater.

"Ya?"

"Let's go bury the bird before Mom gets up."

Matt looked at his watch. "It's not even six o'clock!" he said, scowling at his sister.

"I know," she said. "Where's the bird?"

"Over there," Matt said. "On the desk."

Jeannie walked over and pushed the clothes aside. "I'll go tape up the box while you get dressed," she said.

"You mean you're going to bury the whole box?" Matt asked. "It was just opened!"

"You don't think anybody wants to blow their nose on tissue a bird died on, do you?" And Jeannie walked out.

As the sun rose above the horizon, Matt dug a little hole in front of the bushes under Jeannie's window. Jeannie placed the box in the hole and stood back.

"I wonder if dead birds sing when they go to heaven," she said quietly. Matt looked up at her. What a weird thing to say, he thought.

"I wonder if they even go to heaven," Jeannie continued. She looked up at the sky. "I just hope this robin's little babies don't starve now." Matt hadn't even thought of that. He pictured a nest full of baby robins, mouths gaping, waiting for food.

"OK, Matt," Jeannie said, sniffling. "Go ahead and bury it. But somehow I think birds should be buried in the clouds, not on the ground."

Matt shoveled dirt onto the box, shaping a little mound where the hole had been. He patted it lightly with the back of the shovel.

"Someday that will happen to all of us," Jeannie said, dramatically. She ran inside, clutching a tissue, crying.

*　　*　　*

"Anybody home?"

Matt looked up and saw Scott, dressed in a tie and coat, standing in the door. Scott's hair was still wet from a morning shower, and Matt could smell Scott's after-shave all the way across the room.

"Hi," Matt said.

"You're looking better," Scott said, reaching up and adjusting his tie. "Better than what, I don't know." He smiled. "How are you feeling?"

"Pretty good," Matt said.

"I'd, um, I'd like to talk with you just a moment," Scott said, sounding suddenly like the lawyer he was. He walked up to the bed. "Mind if I sit down?"

Matt moved his legs to one side and nodded his head.

"Matt," Scott said. He sounded more like himself and he took a deep breath, clasped his hands and rested his elbows on his thighs. "When your parents were expecting you, we lived next door to them. I was a high school chum of your dad's, and Judy and I considered your folks our best friends." He looked up at Matt and back down to his hands.

"Well, when they found out that you were coming they asked us to be your godparents. Of course we were delighted." He smiled. "About that time your father was sent to fight in the war and, when he died, we all took it very hard. For a while your mother and sister even moved in with us. But the shock was too much and she had you two months early." He smiled sadly at Matt. "You see, we were expecting Jamie about the time you were supposed to come." He looked at Matt. "But like a lot of things, you were just faster than ol' Jamie.

"Well, the long and short of it is, your mother asked us again after you were born if we'd take care of you if anything happened to her." Scott's calm suddenly disappeared for a second and he fought to keep his upper lip from trembling. "We never dreamed all of this would happen, Matt. But we loved your mother and father and" — he paused, looking straight at Matt — "if you want to, we'd like you to join our family."

He wiped his mouth. His hand was shaking slightly. Matt looked up and saw Judy standing in the doorway.

"Think about it, Matt," she said quietly. "We'll never be like your mother, or your father, but we'll do the best we can." Tears welled up in her eyes.

Matt looked at Scott and Judy and back to Scott. "What will happen to Jeannie?" he asked quietly.

"If she wants to," Scott answered, "we'd love to have her live with us too."

Matt nodded his head. "If Jeannie comes home today, where will she stay?"

"I'll move my loom out of the study," Judy said. Scott nodded his head. "She won't be coming home today. But when she does, she'll have a place."

"Well, think about it, Matt," Scott said, getting up. "If Jamie hasn't gone off to school, I've got to take him and then get to work. Just try to relax today. I'm sure Jamie will cause enough trouble at school today for both of you." He smiled.

I wonder how Jamie will like having a sister, Matt asked himself as Judy and Scott left the room. And an older sister, to boot.

Eight

cott left for work and Jamie left for school, leaving a quiet emptiness behind him. After a few minutes, Judy came back in with the breakfast tray. "The way you and Jamie were carrying on this morning I figured this might be my last chance to serve you breakfast in bed." She put the tray on his lap. "You do look like you're feeling fine."

"I am," Matt said. He gulped down the orange juice and chomped into a piece of toast. "Hey, when do I see the doctor?" he asked, spraying bread crumbs on the tray.

"Nine-thirty," Judy said. "I'll get everything ready while you finish breakfast." She looked down at Matt, a big smile on her face. She bent down, squeezed Matt's head between her hands, and planted a big kiss on his forehead. She stood up.

"Does Jeannie know I'm coming?" Matt asked. He was hungry and he took another huge bite of toast. "Boy, I bet she'll be surprised," he mumbled, his mouth full of toast.

Judy's smile dissolved. Her shoulders drooped slightly. "Matt, she's hurt very badly. She isn't even awake yet from the accident."

Matt swallowed the lump of half-chewed toast. Sharp pieces scraped going down. "What's wrong with her?" he asked, frowning. "Everybody says she's badly hurt. But what does that mean?"

"I don't know exactly," Judy said. "She's in critical condition. That's all I really know." She turned to go, but not before Matt saw a hint of tears in her eyes.

I hope she's awake when we get there, Matt thought; I'll try to cheer her up with a good joke or two.

Matt finished his breakfast and got up. He put the tray on the desk and quickly put on his clothes. Matt had always felt comfortable walking around his house without clothes because he'd always done it. In fact, his mother often told him how tired she got putting clothes on him when he was a toddler. But things were different at the Fletcher house. Matt got the feeling that Judy and Scott and Jamie were more modest.

He was combing his hair with his fingers, looking into the mirror over Jamie's dresser, when Judy walked in.

"You're ready!" She was surprised.

"No," he said with a smile. "I'm Matt."

The ride to the hospital was scary to Matt, but not as scary as the ride from the hospital had been. He tensed whenever a car came at them. But Judy was more confident than before, which made Matt more confident too.

During the ride, Matt looked out the window at the melting snow. "Spring teasers," his mother called these kinds of days. She loved them, especially the spring smells of wet earth. She would often bundle up Matt and Jeannie when they were little and take them on long walks through the woods behind Jamie's house, to the open meadows surrounded by trees.

She would point out the tracks that animals left in the snow — rabbits by the score, tracks that they pretended were fox even though they were probably dog. They saw deer tracks, looking like dainty cow hooves. The tracks of small birds peppered the snow where seeds fell from grasses and low bushes that stuck up through the snow.

As the snow melted, the tracks became less distinct. They could imagine that the tracks were made by unicorns, bears, llamas, kangaroos — even extraterrestrials.

They often rested on a small hill in the middle of a small square pasture completely surrounded by trees. On the top of the hill was a single large oak stump, cut just high enough to sit on. Matt, Jeannie, and their mother would brush off the snow and sit there, scanning the sky for hawks and eagles that lived in the woods and searched the field for mice and rabbits.

The shape of the field always seemed odd to Matt. It was regular as a piece of paper, laid flat on the earth, its edges running north, east, south, and west. It must have been a field once, carved into the forest that grew in the fertile bottom soil deposited by Onion Creek when it rose above its banks. The road leading to it was nowhere to be seen, overgrown and lost. But prairie grass, big blue-stem and little blue-stem, had taken over, growing thick, choking out all other plants, keeping the trees and bushes from sneaking into the field from the crowded forest.

As for the oak tree, perhaps the pioneer farmer left it in the middle of the field when he cleared the land so that he would have something to sit under in the heat of the afternoon, to drink water from the nearby creek, or to think lazy thoughts away from his wife's watchful eye. And perhaps, one year, he'd cut the tree down to make oak floors for his house or to keep its shade from stunting the growth of the corn planted around its base.

Matt's throat tightened and he ached to talk to his mother. He'd never shared those thoughts with her. I wonder if she ever knew how much I liked those walks through the woods, he thought. He could hear her voice in his head saying, "Look at those tracks! They must be elf." Matt wanted to hear her voice now, for real. He turned his head and looked at Judy a moment, blinking back tears. He and Jeannie would hike to that forgotten field when she got better, Matt decided.

"Here we are," Judy said, turning into the large parking lot.

Matt's stomach did a flip-flop as he and Judy walked up to the clinic side of the hospital complex, where all the doctors had their offices. Once he was inside, Matt's stomach tightened even more. Hospitals and clinics try so hard to be clean and odorless, Matt thought, that they smell sick.

After checking with Dr. Woods's nurse and hanging up their coats, Judy and Matt sat down in the waiting room. Judy leafed through some magazines and Matt looked at the other people in the waiting room. One was an old man with a cane and a sour look on his face. Maybe he's here because he's sick of being old, Matt thought. A younger woman was holding a little boy on her lap. Matt wondered why they were at the clinic. They didn't look sick.

"Matthew Smythe," the nurse called.

Matthew and Judy stood up. They followed the nurse

down a corridor when Judy suddenly realized that she was carrying a magazine from the waiting room.

"Oh," she said, stopping. "I better take this back."

Without stopping or looking back, the nurse said, "That's OK. It's probably a year old anyway."

Instead of a stark white examining room, the nurse showed them into a room with wood paneling on one wall and shelves on two walls, packed with books and unruly stacks of papers. Opposite the door was a huge window that looked out into a courtyard with snow-covered bushes and young trees.

The paneled wall was studded with certificates and a few photographs. In front of it was a large desk covered with papers, a stethoscope sprawled on top. The stethoscope didn't look quite up to the job of holding down the piles of paper.

"Please sit down," the nurse said, motioning them to a pair of large chairs facing the desk.

Matt and Judy sat down. The nurse quickly took Matt's blood pressure, pulse, and temperature. She scribbled something on a notepad and then left, closing the door behind her. Judy reached over the arm of her chair and took Matt's hand.

"How do you feel?" she asked, looking at him.

"OK," Matt answered.

"I wonder . . . ," Judy began. But just then Dr. Woods walked in.

"Good morning," he said, an official-looking smile on his face. He walked over to the desk and, finding a spot bare of papers, he half-sat and half-leaned on the desk top.

He put the folder down by his side and crossed his arms over his chest.

"It's good to see you, Mrs. Fletcher," he said, looking at Judy. She nodded her head. "And Matt, you're looking good. How do you feel?" Without waiting for an answer he uncrossed his arms and stepped toward Matt. "Let's take a look at that shoulder."

Deftly, Dr. Woods slipped Matt's arm out of the sling and began massaging the arm, from Matt's elbow all the way up to his shoulder. Dr. Woods hit a couple of places that were sore near the shoulder. They were sore but not painful, and Matt didn't flinch.

"Any pain?" Dr. Woods asked. He took Matt's elbow in one hand and, holding his shoulder in the other, lifted Matt's elbow so that it was level with Matt's head. Aside from being stiff, Matt felt nothing unusual. He shook his head no.

"Good. Good," Dr. Woods said. He slipped the sling over Matt's head and put it on the desk. "Everything looks good. Any headaches?" Matt shook his head no. "Dizziness?" Again, Matt shook his head no. "How many?" Dr. Woods held up his hands with two fingers showing on one hand and three on the other.

"Five," Matt answered.

"Wrong," Dr. Woods said. "Two. Only two hands — I didn't say fingers." Dr. Woods looked like he wanted to smile at his joke. Instead he glanced over at Judy and then returned his gaze to Matt.

"Matt, could you go back to the waiting room for a couple of minutes? I'd like to talk to Mrs. Fletcher about some things. Let me get you going in the right direction," he said, standing up and walking with Matt to the door. He opened it and they both walked out into the corridor. "Right down there," Dr. Woods said, pointing to the left. "You can't miss it."

Ya, Matt thought. Who would miss this place, anyway? He walked down the hall. All the doors were closed and everything was quiet. When he got to the waiting room he found a young man with long, stringy hair sitting where the old man had been. Maybe the old man grew young, Matt thought. The woman and the little boy were gone, but an older lady was sitting one seat over, reading a book.

Sick people, unhappy people. Everywhere in here, Matt thought. This isn't a very happy place. I hope everybody's being nice to Jeannie.

Matt sat down and picked up a magazine. He was right in the middle of an article on American Indian artifacts when Dr. Woods and Judy walked into the waiting room. Judy's eyes were red, as if she'd been crying. She stood slightly behind Dr. Woods, biting her lower lip.

"Matt," Dr. Woods began, "would you like to see your sister?"

A funny feeling crept into his stomach as he looked at them. Something was wrong. "Yes," he said, "I would."

He stood up and tossed the magazine on the table. He and Judy got their coats and followed Dr. Woods down the hall.

"Your sister is still unconscious," Dr. Woods said as they walked.

The hall was white and tubelike. Occasionally people walked by. Some of them said hello to Dr. Woods. Most of them were in too much of a hurry to say anything.

They came to the end and a white sign with red letters said "Intensive Care." The hallway opened into a large room, partitioned by curtains on shiny silver pipes that snaked along the ceiling. A nurse walked up to them.

"Hello, Dr. Woods," she said.

"Jean Smythe, please," he said.

The nurse led them to the far end of a large room. Matt noticed nurses scurrying around and the noise of pumps and the rhythmic beep of a machine. He didn't hear any voices, only the padding of feet. And it smelled bad, like an outhouse.

"I'll go get her chart," the nurse said.

"Now, Matt," Dr. Woods said, "she was very badly hurt in the car accident. In fact, she won't look very much like your sister at first."

Matt felt like he was walking in a dream. He approached the curtain where his sister was supposed to be. All sounds disappeared, and he reached out to part the curtain. Before he could touch it, Dr. Woods reached over Matt's head and drew the curtain open.

Matt froze. There, on a bed, lay his sister. Her shoulders and head were propped up by pillows. Tubes were going into her nose and into one wrist. A large tube came out of her mouth and led to a gurgling machine by her bed. Everything but her arm and head was covered by a white sheet. The air smelled of dried blood, like breathing in after stopping a bloody nose.

Dr. Woods took Matt's hand and led him to his sister's side. Judy followed close behind. Jeannie's face was bloated. Her eyes were swollen and closed. Her eyelids were bruised and a bruise as big as a saucer encircled each eye. Her nose was bandaged and there were stitches on one cheekbone and on her chin.

Matt looked down the length of her body. The sheet dropped to the bed where one leg should have been. He looked up at Dr. Woods.

"What happened to her leg?" Matt asked, stunned.

"It was badly crushed and we had to amputate," he replied. "The other leg wasn't so bad. But blood isn't circulating in it very well. If it doesn't get better, we won't be able to fight infections and we'll have to amputate that leg too."

Matt was dumbstruck. He stared at his sister. He could hear Judy sniffling behind him.

When people are asleep they look peaceful, Matt thought. But his sister looked unhappy and hurt, like the time she hit her finger with a hammer and refused to cry. Her hair was shaved partway up from her forehead and Matt noticed a long, dark purplish row of puckery stitches stretching over her scalp.

Without thinking, Matt reached out and took his sister's hand. He suddenly felt sorry for all the mean things he'd ever thought about her or said to her. In fact, he hadn't been nice to her in the car after the swim meet, before the . . . accident. Gently, he squeezed her hand. Her eyes flinched and her mouth twitched. Matt dropped her hand quickly. It flopped by the bedside.

"We should leave now," Dr. Woods said, picking up Jeannie's arm and checking the tape that secured the tube. He laid her arm back on the bed. "I'll talk to the nurse for a minute. Can you find your way out?"

Judy shook her head yes. Matt just stood, staring at his

sister, tears coming to his eyes. Slowly he walked up to his sister and, bending over the bed, he kissed her gently on the cheek. He stood up, surprised at what he'd just done. Unless he had to, he'd never kissed her before.

Matt looked at his sister. "Why isn't she awake?" It's been two days since the accident, he thought.

"When people are hurt badly, especially around the head, they sometimes go into a coma — a deep sleep," Dr. Woods said. "Some people think it helps the body repair itself, going into a deep sleep."

Matt looked up at Dr. Woods. "Her leg," he said. "Does it hurt?"

"It's tender to the touch in spots," he said. "But there has been some nerve damage. We just don't know how much of her leg she'll be able to use and how good the feeling will be."

Matt was afraid to ask the next question. But he had to. "When will she wake up?"

Dr. Woods looked at Judy and then at Matt. "We don't know when she'll wake up."

Matt looked over at Jeannie. Wake up, you hear! he said to her silently. You wake up.

Jeannie just lay there.

Matt felt Judy's hand squeeze his shoulder softly. They turned away from the bed and silently walked out of the hospital and into the bright "spring teaser."

"We have one more place to go," Judy said as they pulled out of the parking lot. Matt looked at her. "I'd like to go to your house and get a few more clothes for you and see if everything is all right." Her voice was still trembly.

81

As they drove, Matt looked at people walking on the sidewalk, beyond the row of parked cars to their right. His heart began beating fast and his eyes nearly popped out of his head as he spotted a woman walking ahead, her back to them. Her hair, her coat, they way she was walking — she looked just like his mother!

Matt frantically craned his neck to look at the woman's face as they passed. Crushed, he saw an older, sagging face. He turned back in his seat and stared straight ahead.

Deep in his gut, Matt felt the need to talk to his mother, to feel her hugging him. He pinched the inside of his wrist to keep from crying. But tears dribbled down his face anyway, and onto his parka.

Matt was surprised that the house looked just like it always did. Judy parked the car in the street, and they trudged through the snow on top of the sidewalk. Matt tried to step into the footsteps Judy punched into the snow. He got snow inside his shoes anyway.

"I know it's in here," Judy said, as she fumbled around in her purse for the key. She pulled it out and unlocked the front door. They walked in.

Matt looked around the foyer. Everything looked normal — the boots lined up by the door, the dried grasses in the vase on the living room coffee table, the potted palm in the dining room. But he felt like a stranger in somebody else's house.

"Let's go upstairs and get some clothes for you," Judy said.

I didn't make my bed, Matt suddenly thought as they walked up the stairs. He remembered a big pile of dirty clothes he'd stuffed under his bed before the swim meet. Those were probably the clothes he wanted to take to the Fletchers'. And some of them really smelled.

"Go ahead and get the clothes you want, Matt. I'll check in your mother's room for some papers the lawyers need." Matt watched Judy walk down the hall. Matt could picture his mother's bedroom. Her bed was made and everything was put away. The photograph of his father faced the bed from its place on a chest of drawers.

Matt walked into his room. It was a mess. He reached into his closet, got his knapsack, and began stuffing the dirty clothes from underneath the bed into it. He looked through his drawers and closet and stuffed a few more things into the pack.

Matt looked around the room. If he had died, what would people think about him having a room like this?

He slung the backpack onto his good shoulder and walked to the hallway. Judy was still in his mother's room, rummaging around.

I wonder what Jeannie's room looks like, Matt thought. He opened her door and stuck his head inside. It was definitely a girl's room, he thought. Posters on the wall were fuzzy scenes of couples walking hand-in-hand through forests or on beaches, with cute little sayings printed in the foliage or the sky. Her bedspread was pink with a skirt of ruffles. And her window seat was crowded with pillows.

It was a room that just felt like Jeannie, Matt thought. Clean, crowded, and orderly. No secrets.

But wait, Matt thought. Jeannie had a diary that she kept hidden — under her mattress. From time to time,

Matt had tried to sneak looks at it, but Jeannie had always walked in at the wrong moments.

He pushed the door open and walked up to the bed. She'd never know, Matt thought. He'd put it back before she got out of the hospital. Matt smiled. He would really be able to fight with Jeannie now. He'd know all her secrets, know how to really bug her. He could probably get her to do almost anything if he found the right things to threaten her with. He might even be able to shock her out of her coma, he thought.

He was just about to make his move when he heard Judy's voice right behind him. "We'd better go now, Matt. It's getting late." She walked up to him. "Got everything you need?" Matt nodded his head yes. "Let's leave everything the way it is in here — for Jeannie," Judy said quietly.

They both turned and walked out, closing the door behind them.

Nine

1 *t was oddly sunny and cheerful for a funeral day.* Matt was sitting next to a window in the back of a limousine with Jamie, Judy, and Scott. A somber man in gloves and a cap, from the funeral home, was driving the car slowly behind a hearse with pulled curtains, which carried his mother's body.

Matt's shirt collar pinched his neck. He loosened his tie slightly and undid the top button. Judy had insisted that he wear the tie. Matt looked over to see if she noticed. She was lost in thought, gazing out the window.

Before the short service at the funeral home, Matt searched for a bathroom. He'd been so preoccupied earlier that morning — thinking about his mother and sister and not wanting to wear the clothes he was supposed to wear — that he had completely forgotten about going to the bathroom. He was very uncomfortable when they reached the funeral home. Desperate to find a men's room, he unexpectedly ran into a dimly lit room where a coffin was resting. The coffin was framed by flowers, and the top half of the lid was open.

Matt gasped and forgot his problem. He was looking at

his mother. Her face was pink and lifelike, her hair was neatly combed, her eyes closed as if she was sleeping. Her arms were folded over her stomach.

Matt began to shake. His heart was pounding against his breastbone as he walked up to the casket, to make sure it was really his mother. It was. Close up, her face was waxy in spots and powdery in others. And her nose looked funny — like somebody had molded it out of clay and not gotten it quite right before they stuck it on her face.

Her hands looked real, like the hands he'd held so often when he was scared, the hands that had irritated him by brushing the hair from his forehead, the hands he'd watched countless times washing dishes or fidgeting nervously on the steering wheel.

Matt reached out his hand to touch one of hers. His hand began trembling. He held his breath and closed his eyes. The shaking subsided.

Her hand felt cold and hard. He took a deep breath. The air smelled sickly sweet — a mixture of the fragrant flowers and some other things Matt couldn't place. Maybe that's the smell of death, he thought. Or embalming fluid. Matt stopped breathing deeply.

He opened his eyes and looked into his mother's face. He expected her chest to rise and sink slowly and her eyes to flutter open. He wouldn't have been surprised if she'd smiled, sat up, and said good morning. The longer he touched her, the warmer her hand seemed to get.

Questions began popping into his mind like damp fire-crackers. *Why did you die and leave me alone? How could you do this to me?* He felt a mighty wave of anger rush over him. *How could you leave me with this aching and this hurt?* Angrily Matt squeezed her hand. The wave broke, and spread like hissing foam. And like a wave, the anger subsided. He felt guilty. I should be sad, not angry, he scolded himself. Anger swelled up again in him, this time at himself.

Matt didn't know how long he stared. He was lost in a tangle of thoughts, with no thoughts in particular.

Approaching voices snapped Matt out of his reverie. He quickly took his hand away from his mother's and stepped back from the coffin.

At the same time his bladder shot a warning ache through his body, and Matt realized that he'd have to find a bathroom before he peed in his pants. He jammed one hand in his pant pocket, grabbed hold of himself, and squeezed tight in case he was too late.

Running, Matt narrowly missed two men as he turned down a dim hallway. One of them was Mr. Untterbach. Without looking back, Matt kept running and found a bathroom, just in time.

Standing at the urinal, Matt remembered that when he was small, his mother always took him into the women's bathrooms when he needed to go. Sometimes Jeannie did, too, even though she was never much help. Jeannie couldn't lift him to the sink, turn on the water and help him wash his hands — all at the same time. And she always refused to help him wipe himself.

"Don't touch anything!" his mother would always say as they walked into the bathroom. "There are germs everywhere!" His mother hated public restrooms, which usually smelled like urine mixed with disinfectant. Matt had been so afraid of germs that, to avoid breathing them in, he sometimes took a gulp of air before they went in, and held it as long as he could. He never could hold his breath long enough, though, and he always ended up breathing in the awful, contaminated air. It almost made him sick, just thinking about all the germs that were playing around in his nose and in his lungs.

His mother was very careful not to touch anything with any bare part of her body. She would wipe the toilet seat and then cover it with a layer of toilet paper — sometimes two. And when Matt was finished, she never touched the flush handle with her bare hands. She would grab a wad of tissue and then flush. Or, Matt remembered with amazement, she would hold on to his shoulder, kick up her right leg and flush with the heel of her shoe.

For a long time, going to the women's bathroom didn't bother Matt. If women were waiting for a stall or washing up they almost always fussed over him — telling his mother how cute he was. But one day, Matt decided he was big enough to go by himself into the men's bathroom. His mother tried to talk him out of it, but he marched in anyway.

As Matt flushed, he remembered that first time by himself in the men's bathroom. The urinals were too high for him to use properly. But instead of going back to his mother, he'd just taken aim and let fly. He'd made a mess on the wall and floor, hardly hitting the urinal once.

When he came out, his mother asked, "Well, how'd it go?"

He answered proudly, "It went everywhere!"

* * *

"Where were you?" Judy asked, with a distracted look on her face.

"The bathroom," he answered, equally distracted. He was thinking about his mother.

Matt sat in the front row for the service. To his right sat Judy, Scott, and Jamie. Matt sat one chair over from the aisle. He felt better not sitting on the aisle. He looked over at the chair protectively every time someone walked by. This chair is for Jeannie, he thought. If anybody sits down in it, I'll tell them it's already taken. Jeannie should be here, Matt thought. We should be sitting here together. He closed his eyes and pictured Jeannie dressed for church in some ruffly blue and white dress, crying and sniffling. Matt opened his eyes and looked at the empty chair and tried to imagine her sitting there. All he saw was an empty chair.

The small room filled up quickly. He'd seen many of the people before. The harried funeral director set up more folding chairs. An organ played softly in the background, swelling every once in a while as if it was sighing or yawning.

A few people came up to Matt and told him how sorry they were. A few of them, the old ladies especially, dabbed their eyes with hankies. Matt wanted to cry, but, for some reason, he just couldn't.

Matt was surprised when Mr. Roberts walked up to him. Mr. Roberts was wearing a suit and tie instead of a sport shirt and corduroys. Matt had never seen Mr. Roberts in anything but school clothes, and he looked a little odd.

Mr. Roberts smiled and dropped down so that he was eye-to-eye with Matt. In his easy way, he put a hand on

Matt's knee and said, "It'll be good to see you back in school."

"Thanks," Matt said.

Matt was even more surprised when a young man he'd never seen before came up to him and asked, "You're Matt?" Matt stared. He knew that voice. It was from the hospital! "Had to ask. Never seen you before."

"Bert!" Matt said. Bert smiled and nodded. His glasses slid halfway down his nose.

Bert didn't look anything like Matt expected. Bert had such a rough, old-sounding voice, but he looked like he might be a college student — maybe younger.

"Don't know why I'm here," Bert said, reaching out to shake Matt's hand. "Maybe to celebrate getting out of the hospital." Bert's smile disappeared as he realized what he'd said. He swallowed. "The nurse told me about your mother and, well, I wanted to tell you I hope I didn't offend you talking the way I did." Before Matt could reach up to shake his hand, Bert was away and up the aisle, leaving behind the faint scent of beer.

Matt didn't listen to Mr. Untterbach during the service. But Matt watched as he spoke, noticing the way Mr. Untterbach looked around at people in the room and gripped the lectern tightly with both hands. When he came to juicy words such as "spirit" and "praise," Matt watched the spray from his lips. The Reverend Mr. Untterbach was really revving his engines, he thought.

And now, Matt was riding behind his mother's body, going to the cemetery where she was to be buried, being followed by cars filled with people he didn't know. Judy began sobbing quietly beside him, and Scott put his arm around her shoulder and drew her close. Scott looked over at Matt and forced a smile.

They followed the hearse through the gates of the cemetery. Matt looked out his window at the tombstones. Some of them were tall and ornate. Most were almost flush to the ground and covered with snow. A few of them were old markers with rounded corners, made of limestone. These were chipped, and a few leaned sharply. All of the old markers were difficult to read.

Does anybody remember these people? Does anybody think about them? Matt didn't think so.

The procession wound around to the quiet corner where his father was buried. Beyond the cemetery Matt could see the snow-covered field, jagged corn stubble poking above the snow at wild angles where it hadn't been completely plowed under.

In the corner of the cemetery was a pile of dirt loosely covered with a green canvas. Folding chairs were set up in one short row on a large piece of plywood with curling edges that was covered with peeling green paint. Mr. Untterbach stood next to a rectangular hole in the ground in front of the chairs, hands clasping a Bible in front of him. The hole had a frame around it made of brass tubes. Two men in overalls and old parkas stood out of the way, behind the pile of dirt, leaning against their shovels, trying to look inconspicuous but peering at the people who'd come to the funeral.

The hearse driver got out and opened the back of the hearse. Matt could see the casket with a wreath of flowers on top. The driver of their limousine got out and walked to the back of the hearse. Scott got out and followed. Soon, several more men from the cars behind them were lifting the casket from the hearse and carrying it toward the hole and the brass frame. Trying not to tip or jostle the casket, they placed it on the cloth webbing slung between the sides of the frame.

Matt followed Judy to the row of chairs. Jamie was close behind. People stood behind the row of chairs and the plywood groaned.

Judy was sniffling. Matt stared at the casket as Mr. Untterbach began to speak. Matt tuned him out and pictured his mother inside the coffin, hands folded neatly, hair combed, her nose not quite right. *I wonder what dress she's wearing,* Matt thought. He hadn't noticed when he saw her in the funeral home.

Occasionally, someone behind him would sob or sniffle or blow their noses. One man cleared his throat loudly. Matt heard these sounds and wanted to cry. But he couldn't. *What's wrong with me? Why can't I cry?* Matt felt guilty that everybody was crying except him. *Maybe I'm cold and heartless. Maybe I'm wicked and bad.* Matt tried to force a tear out, and couldn't. He felt guiltier and more miserable than ever.

Matt thought about his sister a moment. *She doesn't even know this has happened.* Matt pictured her leg and her face, full of pain.

"Amen." Mr. Untterbach ended the service solemnly and dramatically. He stepped away from the coffin and walked to where Matt was sitting. Judy, Scott, and Jamie stood up.

"Thanks, Mr. Untterbach," Scott said. He sounded sad and tired.

Matt just sat and stared down at the coffin. People were walking toward the cars, talking softly, and the two men with shovels came out from behind the pile of dirt. They hesitated for a moment, looking at Matt and the Fletchers. But one of them began uncovering the dirt and the other slowly walked toward the hole.

"Matt." He felt a hand on his shoulder. "Matt, let's go." Matt looked up at Judy's face, streaked with tears.

"No," Matt said. He turned toward the casket. It wasn't over, Matt thought. She hasn't been buried.

"Matt, please." Judy's voice was pleading.

Matt stared straight ahead. He didn't want to leave his mother until she was buried. He wanted to be sure these men were quiet and respectful. "No," he said quietly. Judy took her hand from his shoulder and stepped back.

The man near the casket started a machine that slowly lowered it into the ground. Matt watched in horror as the coffin disappeared from view, leaving a gaping hole. Now they are together, Matt thought, my mother and my father. In boxes, side by side, unable to touch or hold hands or talk to each other. Both of them are lying on their backs, looking upward through closed eyes — seeing nothing.

The men began shoveling dirt from the pile into the hole. Matt heard it thunk hollowly as it hit the casket.

"Matt," Judy said. She stepped forward, took his hand and helped him stand. Matt felt numb all over as he walked beside her toward Scott and Jamie, who were waiting by the limousine.

93

That night, at dinner, conversation was strained, as if everybody was tiptoeing around what they were thinking, trying not to say anything wrong or painful. Matt was quiet, going through the motions of eating. He wasn't tasting anything and couldn't remember from one bite to the next what he'd put into his mouth.

Soon it was time for bed. Matt felt very tired as he got ready. Judy and Scott said goodnight and Jamie stayed to put on his pajamas.

An awkward silence filled the room. Finally, Jamie cleared his throat and said, "Matt, if a girl puts her clothes in a dresser, what does a boy put his clothes in?" Matt looked at Jamie, his mind completely blank.

"A closet?" he asked.

"No," said Jamie. "A dress-him." He smiled but he looked scared. "Matt," he finally said, "Saturday Dad's putting up the bunk beds. Do you want the top or the bottom?"

"The top," Matt said without thinking. Once, at summer camp, Matt had slept in a bottom bunk. All night he had lain awake, terrified that the beds would collapse and fall on him. He'd slept on the top bunk after that.

"You can't top that," Jamie said. His jokes were strained and lifeless, like baby food. "Well, goodnight. See you in the morning." Jamie stood up, gathered his clothes into his arms, and walked to the door. "Want the light out?"

"Thanks," Matt said and, click, it was dark. Jamie pulled the door shut behind him.

Thunk! Thunk! Matt tensed. He heard it again. Thunk! It was the sound of dirt hitting his mother's coffin.

Matt opened his eyes. Darkness was all he could see. The darkness was close, like the darkness in a box or — Matt shuddered — in a coffin. Matt wanted to reach out and feel the darkness, push it away. But he couldn't move.

Thunk! Thunk! Panicking, Matt felt a weight on his chest. He couldn't breathe. He opened his mouth and gasped. Thunk! Thunk! Matt broke into a cold sweat. He struggled to move his hands. He tried to breathe out. Matt closed his eyes and suddenly the room was filled with a piercing shriek.

Footsteps bounded up the hall, the door flew open and Matt felt himself being picked up in strong arms.

"OK, Matt. You're OK." Matt heard Scott's voice close to his ear. And slowly Matt's stiff body relaxed and his breathing became more regular.

Matt opened his eyes. Standing in the doorway, the hall light hitting his face, was Jamie — wide-eyed, mouth open. Matt closed his own eyes and slowly fell asleep.

Ten

*M*att woke up squinting out the window of Jamie's bedroom. He was surprised to see Scott, right outside the window. Scott looked like he was floating in air with a string of Christmas tree lights wound loosely around his shoulder. He was untangling a knot of cord and lights. Knot untangled, Scott looked up and saw Matt staring at him. He smiled.

Matt jumped out of bed and grabbed his underwear off the floor. He hurried toward the window, trying to stick his feet in the underwear and run at the same time. His elbows pointed everywhere and he felt like a demented duck. Pulling his underwear up with one hand, he unlatched the window with the other and, with both hands, heaved it up. A blast of cold air hit him and goosebumps sprang up all over his body.

"Hi, sport," Scott said, bending down slightly and talking through the open window. "Thought I'd leave these up 'til next Christmas, but Judy wouldn't hear of it."

Matt tried to keep warm by crossing his arms and holding his shoulders. He bent forward and looked out the window. "You're on a ladder!" he said.

"I'm not standing on air!" Scott said, laughing.

Matt heard the scraping sound of a snow shovel on cement and, sticking his head out the window a little farther, he spotted Jamie touching up the shoveling he'd done after the last snow. "Hey, Jamie!"

"Whoa!" Scott said, letting go of the cord he was holding and grabbing the window ledge. "Careful!"

Jamie looked up. "Hey, Matt." He leaned on the shovel and began laughing. "Now's a good time to ask Dad for your allowance. Just grab the ladder and push. . . ."

"OK. OK," Scott said. "You've got to make allowances for situations like this. I know I'm a pushover. Five dollars a week and not a penny less. Now, Matt, please close the window before you turn into an ice cube. I think Judy has some breakfast for you."

Matt shut the window and trotted toward the pile of clothes at the foot of his bed. He slid to a stop and looked over his shoulder at the window. Scott's face was puckered as he tried to untangle another snarl in the lights. Matt sidled back to the window and, just as Scott looked up in surprise, Matt grabbed the cords and snapped the curtains shut.

He smiled as he walked toward his clothes. The day was off to a sunny start. But as he dressed, Matt's thoughts got darker and thicker and, like coming rain, Matt felt tears building. He didn't know exactly why. It irritated him, but lately he got sad and he cried at unexpected times and for no reason in particular.

As he walked down the stairs, the breakfast smells got stronger. His mother in her coffin at the funeral home flashed in Matt's mind like lightning. His stomach growled like distant thunder and tears began to fall. He almost expected to hear his mother's voice float up from the kitchen. That's silly, he thought. She's dead. Instead he heard Judy singing to herself.

A thought jolted him and he froze, mid-step, on the stairs, his head buzzing. *What will Jeannie think when she wakes up?* She'll probably try to wiggle her toes. *What will she do when she finds out she doesn't have toes?* She'll call for our mother. *What will she do when she finds out our mother is dead?* It was too horrible to think about. Matt bit his lower lip and continued slowly down the stairs.

Judy stopped singing as Matt walked into the kitchen. She put down the bowl she was carrying and walked over to him. "Good morning, Matt," she said. She sounded concerned. "How are you this morning?"

"Fine," Matt said. He looked up at Judy. Her face was like the sun breaking through thunderclouds. He began to feel better. Matt took a deep breath. "I hope you know there's a nut outside taking lights off your house," he said.

Judy looked relieved. "So Scott woke you up," she said. "I told him to wait until you got up."

"He wanted to wait a couple of Christmases," Matt said.

Judy smiled. "What would you like for breakfast? Bacon, ham, sausage?"

"Steak," Matt replied. "Raw. But if you don't have steak, toast and cereal will do."

Matt bolted his breakfast. The excitement he had felt when he got up was returning, and he was eager to get outside, into the sun and the cold air.

"Be sure to wear your mittens," Judy called as Matt rushed out of the kitchen.

He shot out the door and ran smack into a wall of light — ricocheting from the brilliant white snow up into the clear blue sky and back again. Blinded for a moment, Matt skidded to a stop and blinked, looking for a patch of dark or shadow, anything to relieve the glare. Out of the corner of his eyes he saw something scurry behind the dark shape of a large oak tree. It was Jamie.

I'll show him, Matt said to himself. He won't surprise me. Casually, Matt turned his back to the tree. He bent down, pretending to look underneath a bush next to him, and scooped up some snow. In the back of his mind, he pictured Jamie's head poking from one side of the tree and then the other, first low and then high. As he patted the snow into a hard ball, Matt looked up at the sky and counted to ten. I'll plaster him and run around the house, he thought.

Just as he got to ten and was tensing to twirl around and bomb Jamie, Matt heard a noise above him, toward the house. Startled, he looked up just in time to see a snowball arching toward him. He ducked and the snowball skimmed over his right shoulder.

"Gotcha!" Scott yelled from the top of the ladder. Snow from the roof had melted and slid down to the gutter, right above Scott's head. Scott reached up for more snow.

Matt quickly ran toward the nearest tree as the snowball flew by. It hit the sidewalk next to his feet with a "blat."

Too late, Matt realized he was running toward the tree that Jamie was hiding behind. "Surprise!" Jamie yelled, stepping out from behind the tree. Matt jumped sideways, but Jamie's snowball hit his leg. Remembering the snowball in his hand, Matt drew back and fired in Jamie's direction.

"Surprise yourself!" he yelled. The snowball hit Jamie square in the chest.

Matt veered out of Jamie's way and ran toward the house. Right in front of him, leaning against the house, was the snow shovel Jamie had been using moments before. Matt grabbed it. I'll bury both of them, he thought gleefully. He turned and saw Jamie reach back to throw another snowball. Without thinking Matt held the shovel over his face. The shovel jumped and twisted as the snowball smacked into it.

Matt lowered the shovel and laughed at Jamie's surprised face. Scooping up some snow, Matt charged toward Jamie. He held the shovel in front of him, trying to balance the snow. It was tricky and, before he knew it, he stumbled and fell face-first into the snow. The shovel went flying off to the side.

"Aha!" Jamie yelled, triumph in his voice. He sprang toward Matt and skidded to a stop on his knee right next to him. He scooped up some snow and began stuffing it down Matt's neck.

"Hey, no fair!" Matt yelled, turning to Jamie and plastering a handful of snow into Jamie's laughing face. Jamie's mouth was wide open and Matt was pleased that most of the snow was now crammed inside.

"Zbrygnaluf!" Jamie grunted, spitting snow and trying to talk at the same time.

"Don't talk with your mouth full," Matt shouted, scrambling to his feet. He plastered another handful of snow onto Jamie's face and rubbed it in. Matt ran around the tree and bent down to scoop up more snow. He loved a good snowball fight and he loved it even more when he was winning. "Yippee!" he laughed and he turned to throw his snowball at Jamie.

To his surprise, Jamie was only a few feet away, a snowball raised in his hand. Jamie's face was red and scrunched with effort as he threw the snowball as hard as he could. Matt closed his eyes and tried to shield his face. But it came too fast.

The snowball hit, jerking Matt's head back. Matt's face felt like it had been sliced with tiny pieces of ice. His eyes teared as he opened them and looked into Jamie's contorted face.

Jamie's mad! Matt was so shocked and surprised that he just stood stupidly and watched Jamie breathing hard, getting redder by the second. Without warning a snowball grazed Matt's shoulder, getting snow onto his neck and into his coat. He looked up and saw Scott, smiling and laughing at the top of the ladder. "Gotcha again!" he yelled.

Jamie grunted, grabbed Matt's coat, and heaved him to the ground. "I'll clean your dirty face!" he sputtered, and he jumped on top of Matt.

"Hey, guys. This is fun. Let's not act like adults," Scott called to them. "Jamie, be careful!" Scott began scrambling down the ladder as Jamie plastered a handful of snow onto Matt's face and ground it in with all of his weight. Matt yelped in pain and wriggled out from under Jamie.

"Now, boys," Scott said jumping off the ladder and struggling to extricate himself from the lights. "Jamie!"

Tears of pain and anger and confusion were trapped behind Matt's closed eyes. His eyes felt like they were going to burst. Matt staggered to his feet. "I hate you!" he shouted in Jamie's direction. His voice was thick and ugly. He turned and opened his eyes. Home, he thought, tears streaming down his face. *I want to go home!*

He began to run across the yard when it struck him as if he'd run into a brick wall. He couldn't go home. His mother was dead!

All of the energy left his legs and Matt crumpled into a heap in the snow. He sobbed, his forehead buried in the snow.

Matt felt hands on his shoulders, lifting him gently up. "Matt, it's all right."

"I ... want ... to ... go ... home ...," Matt blubbered. He began to sob even harder.

Quietly and firmly, Scott said, "Matt, this is your home. You are home. This is your home and we love you."

Matt looked up. Tears were streaming down Scott's face.

"Jamie didn't mean it," Scott said.

"I did too," Jamie seethed.

Matt and Scott looked up in surprise.

"You think you're so tough all the time," Jamie yelled. "You always have to win! You've always got to be on top! I've had it!" He quivered with anger. Matt and Scott didn't move from where they were. "Go home! See if I care!" Jamie glared at Matt. "Maybe I can have my parents back!"

Matt was stunned. Sniffling, he tried to brush tears from his own eyes with the back of his mittened hand. He got an eyeful of snow. Matt began to cry again.

"Jamie, listen to me," Scott said, helping Matt to his feet. "We are all one family now. Matt and you are going to have to share one set of parents. There are just two of us, I know, but I think there's enough love and time to go around in this family." He looked at Matt and back to

Jamie. "You two have complaints about not getting enough attention, either of you, you come to me or Judy. You *don't* take it out on yourselves. Understand?"

Jamie had never heard his father talk like that before. Matt stared wide-eyed. Scott normally handled problems so cleverly. They both shook their heads.

"Good," Scott said. His voice was kinder, and once again tears came to his eyes. "Come here, you two. I've got a million hugs I've got to use up today or lose them. And I can't think of two people I'd rather give them to right now."

Matt began to shiver as the snow caught in his shirt collar began to melt and drip down his back. Arm-in-arm-in-arm, Scott and Jamie and Matt walked silently to the house.

"You guys better go up and change," Scott said, opening the door for them. "But don't change too much — I love you just the way you are."

In a few minutes Scott came bounding up the stairs. He was singing at the top of his lungs. "There's *snow* business like *snow* business than *snow* business I know!"

He swooped into the room and stopped singing. Both Matt and Jamie looked up from the bed where they were putting on dry socks.

Jamie turned to Matt and said, "Should we call the police or ignore him and hope he goes away?"

"Let's see what the poor man wants. Maybe he's lost and needs a dime to call home," Matt said.

"Well," Scott said, feigning injury. "I guess the bunk beds can wait."

103

Jamie jumped up. "Oh no! Really?" He turned to Matt. "Let's help him bring up the bunk beds."

Matt's face still tingled from the fight, but he grinned. "There goes the neighborhood!" he said, throwing both hands up in the air.

"Hey, Jamie," Matt asked as they were getting ready for bed. "Do you remember the time we walked in on my mother when she was taking a bath?"

Jamie yanked off a sock. "Ya. When we were three or four? Was she ever surprised!"

Matt took off his shirt, wadded it up into a ball, and shot it, like a basketball, into the closet. "I'll say. She didn't yell at us, though."

"Why did we do that in the first place?" Jamie asked, slipping off his pants and kicking them into the corner with the rest of his clothes. He reached for his pajamas.

"We had to go to the bathroom, I think," Matt said. "My mom just covered her chest with one arm and grabbed a towel and wrapped it around herself as she got out of the tub. We couldn't decide who should go first — I *really* had to go — so she told us to go at the same time and to hurry up."

"Ya, I remember now," Jamie said. "She sat on the edge of the tub and waited for us to finish so she could get back into the water."

"Jamie?"

"Ya?"

Matt giggled. "Do you remember how surprised I was when I saw you . . . your weenie? It sure looked funny to me." Matt burst out laughing.

"Ya, I remember." Jamie snickered. "You pointed and said, 'What happened!' I thought it had turned green or something or was just about ready to fall off."

Matt smiled sheepishly. "Then Mom explained to us about circumcision and how you weren't circumcised and I was."

"She was real nice about it," Jamie said. "But I don't think I really understood. When I went home I told my mother that I wanted to be circumcised just like you, and that night my dad and I had a long talk about boys and girls and babies...."

"And birds and bees!" Matt laughed as he climbed up into his bunk. "I think I was disappointed I wasn't like you." He crawled under the cool sheets.

"Ya, my dad told me it was my 'One-Eyed Trouser Snake'!" Jamie said laughing. "He told me to be careful of it, just like I would any wild animal." They both roared. "Hey Matt, when you have kids and I have kids, you should tell my kids the facts of life and I'll tell your kids the facts of life. It'll be a lot less embarrassing that way."

"Ya," Matt said. "Hopefully by then we'll know the facts of life."

"You know what I remember most, though?" Jamie asked as he walked over to turn out the light. "I remember trying real hard to make the water in the toilet bowl swirl one way and you were making it swirl the other way." Jamie's voice was beginning to lose some of its spark. He turned out the light, walked over to his bed and crawled in.

Matt lay on his back in bed and let his eyes get used to the dark. The dark and the shadows made the ceiling look farther away than it really was. Just to be sure, Matt reached up and touched the ceiling with the tips of his fingers. "Hey, Jamie."

"Huh?" Jamie grunted.

"Goodnight."

"Goodnight," Jamie said through a yawn.

"Jamie?"

"Ya?"

"Don't snore." Matt felt the mattress jump. He leaned over and looked down. In the dark he saw that Jamie's leg was straight up and his foot pushed against the wire mesh holding Matt's mattress.

"That's what I'll do if *you* snore," Jamie said. "Or if you wet the bed and I get rained on." Jamie let his leg fall down and rolled over. Tomorrow I'll have to remember to hide a glass of water up here, Matt thought. He pounded his pillow into a comfortable shape and fell asleep smiling.

Eleven

*M*att felt as nervous as the first day of school. The night before, he had spent hours tossing and turning, straining to sleep. That had only given him a headache and made falling asleep impossible. When he finally dozed off, his dreams were restless and disturbing — walking into a classroom full of kids and realizing that he had no clothes on, talking and having all of the words come out backward, being attacked by dogs on the way to school.

Jamie had a hard time waking up. "Did you win?" he asked through a huge yawn. They were getting dressed for school.

"Win what?" Matt asked, puzzled.

"The wrestling match you had last night with that gorilla," Jamie replied. "You kept mumbling in your sleep and the bed creaked so much I thought I was on the *Mayflower* during a storm." Matt had just missed a week of American history concentrating on the Pilgrims.

"Sorry," Matt said. "I kept having weird dreams."

"Musta been some gorilla," Jamie mumbled, pulling on a sweater.

Judy pushed them to eat breakfast fast and to get out the door.

"Trying to egg me on?" Jamie quipped as she put a plate of scrambled eggs in front of each of them before they even sat down.

"A toast!" Judy said, holding up a piece of toast and waggling it like an index finger. Butter dripped onto the table. "A toast to two boys who better hurry or they'll be late for school."

Jamie took the toast from his mother. "Get me out of this jam!" he said, glopping raspberry preserves on the toast and destroying it in three huge bites.

Matt was too nervous to join in the usual breakfast jollies of the Fletcher household. He just chewed and, every once in a while, remembered to swallow. He didn't want to go back to school. He felt the same as he had the year his mother told the barber to cut his longish hair very short just a few days before school was out for the summer. He could never figure out why she didn't wait until summer vacation.

"Wooh, we're going to be late if we don't hurry up," Jamie said, looking at his watch. Judy handed them their coats and lunches as they got up from the table.

"Hurry now," she said. "And take care."

The cold air felt good. Matt breathed it in deeply as he and Jamie trotted down the sidewalk toward school. No other kids were in sight, a sure sign that they were either late for school or way too early. Matt knew they weren't too early.

The bell began ringing just as Matt and Jamie rushed into the school building and raced down the dark hall toward their homeroom. They skidded to a stop, hoping nobody had seen them running, and threw their coats and lunches into Jamie's locker, which was closer to Room 5. The bell stopped just as they rushed, breathlessly, into the brightly lit classroom.

All faces turned to them. So much for slipping in quietly, Matt thought.

Mr. Roberts was sitting on his high stool at the front of the class. He was shuffling papers, getting ready to read the school announcements. Matt's heart was pounding. He took a deep breath and walked quickly to his desk in the back row, pretending that nothing was unusual. Jamie scurried to his in the front.

"Sorry we're late, but . . . ," Jamie chattered.

"That's quite all right, Jamie," Mr. Roberts said. "We were just about ready to begin." He looked up at Matt. "We're glad to have you back, Matt." He cleared his throat and looked at the clipboard in his hand. "This is how our day is stacking up," he said. "I hate to talk about this first thing this morning, but the principal has unmistakable evidence that some students have been smoking in the bathrooms. Don't make us put smoke detectors in the stalls . . ."

Matt was relieved that Mr. Roberts hadn't said anything about his mother and sister. He got out his math book. One nice thing about having Mr. Roberts for homeroom was not having to move for his first-period class — math. Matt looked over at Melanie, who sat at his right. How many times will she go to the girls' room today? he wondered. Melanie turned her head and stared at him coolly, daring him to keep looking. Matt blushed and quickly turned back to his math book. The bell rang and everybody got out their books.

Usually Matt was lost in math. Today he was lost in thought. Mr. Roberts chatted with the class about fractions, drawing pies on the board and letting the class decide what flavor the pie should be. Matt found himself doodling on a piece of paper, drawing tombstones. Some of them were tall and elaborate with carved squiggly designs. Some of them were small, plain, flat on the ground. Several had his name on them. Others were blank.

Matt looked around the classroom. Frank was the biggest, most awkward kid in the class. Matt decided that Frank would probably like an inconspicuous tombstone when he died. Matt wrote Frank's name in simple block letters on a low, flat, plain tombstone.

He looked over at Carol, who was bent over her desk furiously scribbling a note to pass to one of her friends — if Mr. Roberts didn't get it first. Carol was always chewing gum, which was against school rules. She was caught every day and every day she was genuinely puzzled by how the gum got in her mouth. She popped it in each morning when she got up and then forgot about it.

Carol never forgot about roller skating, though. She was a championship roller skater and often brought newly won trophies to class. "Some day roller skating will be an Olympic event," she told the class once, chewing furiously on her gum. "And I'm gonna be ready."

Matt wrote Carol's name on a large tombstone that looked like a trophy. He decorated it with a single high-topped skate.

Matt watched Mr. Roberts, happily drawing pies on the

chalkboard and letting different kids go up and divide them up in different ways. Matt looked at the tombstones he'd drawn on the piece of paper. None of them seemed to fit. Chewing on the end of his pencil, Matt tried to think of one that would.

He began to draw furiously, totally absorbed. He drew a craggy boulder with a smoothed oval on its face for the name. He was just putting the final touches on Mr. Roberts's name when he felt a hand on his shoulder. He jumped.

"Matt, we're getting a head start on tomorrow's math homework," Mr. Roberts said softly. He pointed to the tombstone with his name on it. "That's nice. Really nice. Did you draw one for yourself?" Mr. Roberts knelt down so that they were eye-to-eye.

"All of these were mine, but somehow they didn't fit," Matt whispered.

"I've sometimes thought about what my grave will look like," Mr. Roberts said. Pointing to the picture Matt had just drawn, he said, "You know, *that's* the kind of tombstone the poet Ralph Waldo Emerson has marking his grave. I've always liked Emerson."

Matt didn't know who Emerson was, but he was relieved that Mr. Roberts wasn't upset that he'd been drawing tombstones and putting names on them.

"Let me show you some of the pages you missed in math last week," Mr. Roberts said. "Then I'll let you get back to your work." He looked at Matt and winked.

As the morning dragged, the clock seemed to slow down. As hard as he tried, Matt couldn't do the fraction problems in the book. He couldn't concentrate. He found himself doodling, drawing tombstones in the margins of his paper and letting his mind wander.

He was grateful when recess finally came. Jamie was pulling on his coat as Matt walked up to the locker. "I'll grab a soccer ball," Jamie said, rushing off down the hall.

"But there's snow outside," Matt said.

"That'll make it more fun," Jamie called over his shoulder.

Matt meandered down the hall. He was the last one out the door. The seventh-grade class, as usual, was scattered all over the playground, clumped in little knots. A few girls were standing on the asphalt talking and jumping up and down to keep warm. A couple of boys were building a snowman. Next to them, along a fence separating the schoolyard from a neighbor's yard, another group of boys teased a yapping dog that was frantically trying to get at them through the fence. Several kids were sitting on the swings, and a bunch were out on the field, running after the soccer ball. Matt walked over to the field and stood watching. It was difficult to see who was on what team. Everybody just seemed to be chasing the ball, trying to get in a hard kick as it zigzagged up and down the field. The action came toward him.

"Hey, Smythe," George yelled at Matt. George thought of himself as the coolest kid in the seventh grade. So did the girls. "How'd your old lady look after the crash?" George kicked the soccer ball hard into Matt's chest.

Matt was shocked. He didn't know what to say.

George swaggered toward Matt and picked up the ball.

Everybody else gathered around. George sneered. "I heard she was drunk as a skunk!"

"She was not!" Matt said. Red flashed through his neck and face. He saw Jamie move into a position right behind George.

"You calling me a liar?" George asked.

"Ya, he is," said Jamie, right into George's ear.

George turned to look at Jamie. "You stay out of this, shitface." He turned back to Matt. "Everybody knows." His voice was icy cold.

"Come on, George," Frank said. "Stop picking on him. How would you feel if your old lady just kicked off?"

"Pretty damn good," George said.

"Let's play soccer," said Frank. He walked up to George and grabbed at the ball.

George jerked it away. "This punk just called me a liar," he said. "Didn't you?" He drilled Matt with a hateful look.

Matt was so angry that he shook. "I could just kill you," he muttered.

"Just like your old lady tried to kill you?" George cackled.

That was too much. Fists flying, Matt leaped onto George and they tumbled to the snow. George tried to keep his cool and scramble away from Matt. "Can't ya take a joke?" he asked. Matt buried his fist in George's stomach.

"You son of a bitch," Matt hissed. He drew his arm back and cracked George smack in the mouth.

"Hey!" George squeaked. His lip was split and bleeding. "I was just joking," he said, turning his head to avoid being hit again, and tried to get up.

"I'm dying of laughter," Matt wheezed, and he hit George again hard, right on the side of the face.

"Cut that out, you two," Frank said. He grabbed Matt's arm and started to pull him off George.

"Leave him alone," Matt heard Jamie say in a menacing tone of voice. "Let go." Jamie moved over to Frank. Frank was almost a foot taller, but Jamie pushed Frank away anyway. Frank let go of Matt's arm. Matt hit George again in the stomach.

"What are you, his brother or something?" Frank asked Jamie.

"As a matter of fact, I am," Jamie said. "And if you don't let him beat the shit out of George, you'll have to fight me."

Frank laughed. "Looks like we're too late."

Both Matt and George were on their feet. Mr. Roberts had seen the action and come over. He was standing between them.

"I don't want to hear any stories from either of you. So just cool off." His voice was calm but hard as steel. "George, go in and get an ice pack from the office before your lip swells up. If your parents have any questions about how you look, tell 'em to call me." George looked like he might cry. He stamped off, clutching his mouth. Mr. Roberts picked up the soccer ball and tossed it to Frank.

He turned to Matt. "Matt, let's go check out the swings."

The group of kids wandered back to the field and were soon chasing after the ball as if nothing had happened.

"I don't want to know how that started," Mr. Roberts began. "I know you and I know George and I think you probably did what I would have done...under the circumstances."

"Thanks," Matt said. He was still shaking and trying to control his voice. "Why did he say my mom was drunk?"

"I don't know," Mr. Roberts said. "Just being mean. But last week we did talk about what happened to you, Matt. We talked a long time — almost every day. The account in the paper said that the man who ran into you was charged with drunk driving." Matt stared straight ahead. He could see the man's hateful face. He started shaking again.

"You know how George listens in class," Mr. Roberts continued. "More words go out of his mouth than go into his ears. Just between you and me, it's a wonder his head isn't completely empty." Mr. Roberts smiled. "But more than that, you got a lot of attention last week. If we weren't talking about you, talking about death, or talking about drunk driving, we were thinking about you. And," he said, putting an arm around Matt, "I think everybody was feeling bad about what happened and hoping that you were OK. Maybe George didn't like everybody paying so much attention to you for a change instead of him."

Matt was astounded. "You mean George is *jealous?*"

"That's one way to look at it." Mr. Roberts gave Matt a little hug with his arm.

They walked to the end of the asphalt and watched a couple of kids swinging on the swings.

"Mr. Roberts?" Matt asked, looking up at his teacher.

"Yes."

"Thanks."

Mr. Roberts winked. "Time to go in," he said, and blew the whistle.

Jamie's mother was waiting to pick them up after school. They were going to visit Jeannie at the hospital. Matt hadn't seen her for almost a week and he was anxious to see her.

"You should have seen Matt cave in George's face today," Jamie said as they tumbled into the car. Judy turned around and looked at them in surprise. "Ooops," Jamie said. He turned to Matt. "Sorry."

"You did *what?*" Judy asked Matt sternly.

"George was saying my mother was a drunk, so I hit him," Matt said.

Judy digested this bit of information. "Good for you," she said. She turned around and began to pull out onto the street. "If his mother calls, I'll give her a piece of my mind."

"You should have seen it, Mom," Jamie chattered. "Matt punched George in the . . ."

"That's all right, Jamie," Judy said. "Spare me the details. Matt, I don't usually like fighting. But sometimes it's the only thing that feels good." She looked at him through the rearview mirror. "*If* you're right and *if* you win." She smiled.

When they got to the hospital, the nurse at the front desk paged Dr. Woods. Within a few minutes he came striding down the hall.

"Hello, Mrs. Fletcher. Hello, Matt," he said. "This must be Jamie."

He reached out and shook Jamie's hand. "I was just

checking on Jeannie," he said, herding them down the hall with his arm. "She's still in Intensive Care and she isn't doing as well as I hoped.

Just before they got to the Intensive Care unit Judy took Jamie's hand and said, "We'll wait for you here, Matt."

Dr. Woods led Matt to a different part of the room than before. "We moved her so that she would be away from so much noise," Dr. Woods explained. "Even though she's been in a coma since she arrived, we believe she may be able to hear noise and find it distressing." He reached out and parted the curtain.

Matt was not prepared for what he saw. It looked like his sister had aged seventy years in the past week. She looked like an old lady. The swelling in her face was gone. Her cheeks were sunken, and her face was chalky white with dark circles under her eyes. She looked fragile and shrunken. Matt was horrified.

"She's lost weight," Dr. Woods said.

Matt stared. "Will she be OK?" he whispered.

"We don't know," Dr. Woods said. He walked up to Jeannie and checked a tube going into her arm. "She suffered some brain damage. How much, we can't say. And she has been running a fever." He turned to Matt. "Matt, I don't know when she'll get better. And if she does get better, she may not be the same sister that you knew before the accident."

Matt felt no urge to touch his sister this time. He was shocked by what he saw — and repulsed.

That night, as he lay in bed, he pictured Jeannie —

helpless, asleep, shriveled, lying in the hospital bed. He knew that she was slowly dying.

"Dying of laughter." The phrase tumbled around in Matt's head. "I'm dying of laughter." He'd said that many times. He'd said it to George just today.

Dying of laughter. That wouldn't be such a bad way to go. And tears streamed down his face.

Twelve

att thought the week would never end. The weekend seemed just as far away one day as it did the next. Matt couldn't concentrate on anything at school and there were times when he was overwhelmed by awkwardness around the kids in his classes. He sensed, too, that there were times when a lot of them felt awkward around him. Matt understood. What do you say to the son of a dead woman, anyway?

Fortunately, Jamie was the same as always. And, unfortunately, so was George. George wasn't awkward. He was just plain nasty.

"How's your old lady?" he asked under his breath every chance he got. "Heard she was so pickled they didn't have to embalm her." It wasn't easy, but Matt just ignored George. Whenever he wanted to punch George in the face, he just walked away. George was picking a fight, and the last thing Matt wanted to do was something George wanted him to do.

If it hadn't been for Ralph, nothing exciting would have happened all week. Ralph called Matt on Thursday night and told him to meet him outside school the next afternoon.

"He didn't even ask me," Matt told Jamie afterward. "He *told* me. And he said you couldn't come along."

"Did he say what he wanted?" Jamie asked.

"No. He just said it was important and that it wouldn't take very long."

"My mother said that she talked to Ralph's mother the other day and that he was acting really strange lately. Maybe I should sneak along behind you and make sure he doesn't do something crazy."

"That's OK," Matt said. "Maybe he just wants to talk about Jeannie."

It was just like in the movies. Matt scurried out of the school building, the bell still ringing, and Ralph was waiting by a tree near the street. He was pretending to mind his own business, looking like the kind of person teachers warned about — the ones who lurk around junior high schools to sell drugs. Matt walked up to him.

"Hi, Ralph," he said.

Without looking at him, Ralph started walking down the sidewalk, away from the direction Matt normally walked. "Jamie gonna trail us?" he asked over his shoulder.

"No," Matt said. "Hey, slow down, will ya?"

"Sure," Ralph said. They were out of sight of the school. He slowed down. "Didn't want the principal to think I was pushing anything," he said. His voice and his face relaxed.

They walked for a couple of minutes in silence. Finally, Ralph cleared his throat. "I miss Jeannie," he said. "How is she?"

Matt looked at his feet. "She's not doing too good," he said.

Ralph looked at Matt. Tears came to his eyes. "Do you know the bastard that ran into you?" he asked. Matt shook his head no. "He lives over here a couple of blocks."

They came to a busy intersection and waited for the light to change. "Me and some buddies have been teaching that bottle-sucker a thing or two."

Matt listened, wide-eyed. He'd never heard Ralph talk like that before. In fact, Matt couldn't remember a single time he'd been with Ralph when Jeannie wasn't around. And Ralph was always a perfect gentleman when he was with Jeannie.

"First thing we did was collect a garbage bag full of dog shit and cover his front steps with it." Ralph smiled. "Some of it was pretty fresh. He slipped down two stairs and *sat* on a pile before he even knew it was there!"

Matt smiled.

"Then we let all the air out of his car tires. He didn't even notice them flapping until he'd shredded them on his rims." Ralph turned left. "Then we lined his driveway and sidewalks with beer bottles — on both sides. It took us all weekend to find enough bottles and it took him ten garbage bags to pick them up."

"When'd you do all that?" Matt asked.

"At night," Ralph said. "Then somebody always spied on him to see what happened." He nodded as they walked by a white house with a big picture window in front and green shingles on top. "That's it. The Porter Palace." He spat out the words. "Tonight we're gonna soap all his windows and put some signs up in his front yard."

Matt stared at the house. His blood boiled to think that

the man who killed his mother lived there. He spat into the front yard as they walked by.

"Do you wanna help tonight?" Ralph asked. They rounded the block and turned in the direction of the Fletchers' house.

Matt thought hard. "I'd like to. But I don't know if I can." Scott and Judy were planning to take them out for dinner.

"Come if you can. We'll meet at Brookside Park at nine. By the baseball diamond."

"Would you put something on a sign for me?" Matt asked.

"Sure. What?"

Matt tried to think of something awful enough. " 'Death to Porter,' " he said.

They walked the rest of the way in silence.

Matt didn't sleep well that night. Part of the reason was the linguini with clam sauce he had for dinner. But mostly he thought about what Ralph had told him.

The next morning Matt reluctantly opened his eyes. Everything was bleary. He closed his eyes and tried to decide what he should wear for school. In a flash he realized that it was Saturday! He didn't have to go to school! His eyes flew open, his mind cleared, and he was suddenly wide awake.

Matt turned his head and looked out the window. His heart sank when he saw low, dark clouds scurrying over the tree tops. The wind blew in gusts, making the naked branches of the trees shake and shiver in the cold. As Jeannie used to say, this was a day for vigorous napping.

Matt leaned over the edge of the bed and peered down

at Jamie. Jamie was curled up, hugging his pillow, breathing deeply.

Matt quietly climbed down from the top bunk. He scooped up his underwear from the floor and stepped into it as he walked toward the door. Sneaking a look over his shoulder, to make sure Jamie was still asleep, Matt tiptoed out of the room and walked stealthily down the hall to the bathroom. He peered farther down the hall to see if Judy's and Scott's bedroom door was closed. It was.

The house was very still. Only the sound of wind gusts ruffled the silence. Matt eased the bathroom door shut and slowly filled a glass with warm water. Taking the glass with him, he walked back to the bedroom as quietly as he had left.

Matt peeked into the room to see if Jamie was still asleep. He was. As silently as a greased snake, Matt sneaked across the room and climbed up onto the top bunk, being careful not to spill any water. The bed creaked, and Matt heard Jamie stir. Matt held his breath, and didn't move a muscle until Jamie's breathing settled back into a slow, relaxed rhythm.

Very carefully, Matt leaned over the edge of his bed. He held the glass a foot from Jamie's head and he tipped it. A few drops of water pattered onto the bed, right behind Jamie's neck. Matt tilted the glass more, and a steady small stream of water hit the growing puddle near Jamie's neck. Water began to flow into the dent Jamie's shoulder made in the mattress. The water crept downward, toward the deeper dent made by Jamie's hips.

Jamie's leg twitched. He clutched at his pillow. Matt poured faster now. The stream became a river. Jamie shuddered and gasped and his eyes flickered open. His hand shot up to the back of his neck and, startled, he looked up.

"What the . . . ," Jamie said, his eyes narrowing. He quickly reached his hand to the small of his back and felt the bottoms of his pajamas. "I'm wet!"

"Surprise!" Matt said, smiling from ear to ear. He dumped the rest of the water right on Jamie's face.

"Why, you little rat!" Jamie sputtered, shaking the water from his face. "I'll get even with you, Matt," he said with a chuckle.

"Even with me?" Matt asked. "Are you talking height or IQ? Either way you don't have a chance."

"How will I explain this to Mom?" Jamie giggled.

"Just tell her you peed in your pants."

"Ya, sure," Jamie said. "I was putting fires out in my sleep." He laughed and crawled out of bed. "Ooo, it's been a long time since I've worn wet pajamas." He paraded around the room, pulling out both sides of the pajamas like little tents. He wrestled out of the wet bottoms and, without warning, heaved them at Matt. They missed, smacking the wall right above Matt's head.

The restless, windy weather made both Matt and Jamie restless. At breakfast, Matt took a bite of scrambled eggs and discovered a piece of paper in the lump.

"Where did this come from?" Matt asked, pulling the paper out of his mouth.

Judy stared. "Is that paper?" She couldn't believe her eyes.

Matt looked over at Jamie, who was fighting a smile. A snicker bubbled up, incontrollably. Judy turned to Jamie.

"Jamie, do you know anything about this?" she asked.

"Yes," Jamie said, fighting laughter. "Looks like some chick is writing Matt notes."

For Judy, the snowballs in the refrigerator freezer were the last straw. She called Matt and Jamie into the kitchen, opened the freezer, and pointed at the snowballs.

"Where did these come from?" she asked, looking first at Matt and then Jamie.

"Ever hear of the Cold War?" Jamie asked, looking at the snowballs.

"Jamie, don't get smart with me!" Judy was having a difficult time sounding stern.

"You don't have to worry about Jamie getting smart with anybody," Matt said. "Actually, we were thinking of making chocolate-covered snowballs."

"Tell her the truth, Matt," Jamie said. "Never mind. I'll tell her." Jamie looked at his mother. "We're trying to set an example for the United States and Russia by showing them how to put a freeze on weapons." Jamie snickered.

"That's nice," Judy said. "Now get them out of here. If you hurry, you may even have time to go see a movie."

"A movie?" Jamie exclaimed. "Oh boy!" He grabbed two snowballs and ran for the back door.

"Don't eat too much popcorn," Judy said as they walked out the door. "I have a special dinner planned for tonight."

"Pork lips and chicken feet?" Jamie called over his shoulder.

"No, chicken lips and pork feet," Judy called and then closed the door.

The cold wind nipped their noses as Matt and Jamie hurried along the street.

"Insult me! Insult me!" said Jamie. "I wouldn't mind getting hot and bothered right now. Especially hot."

"No," said Matt. "I never insult ugly people."

"Being ugly, you know how they feel, eh?" Jamie scuffed his shoes along the pavement.

"Know how they feel?" Matt asked. "I never get close enough to people as ugly as you to feel them! That's a disgusting thought."

They rounded the corner and stopped in their tracks. The movie theater was at the other end of the block. But the line came almost to the corner where they were standing. And then it doubled back.

"I've never seen the line wrap around like that," Matt said.

"We'll never get in." Jamie was crestfallen. Some of their classmates had seen the movie five or six times. It was the only thing people talked about at school. Even Mr. Roberts had seen it twice. Matt and Jamie hadn't seen it once.

They turned to go back home.

"There's nothing to do at home," Jamie said. "I wish Dad wasn't at his office. He might have some ideas."

"We could go to my house," Matt said quietly. "I have some games and stuff. I've been wanting to go there anyway."

"I think we should tell Mom first," Jamie said.

"She doesn't need to know," Matt said. "You don't have to tell her everything, do you?"

Jamie looked down at his feet. "OK. But we have to be

home by four. I hope they don't ask us anything about the movie."

They turned onto Matt's street. Matt's house was just a few houses down from the corner. They stopped in front of it. Matt studied the house. He almost expected his mother to open the front door and tell them she had hot chocolate waiting for them in the kitchen. He wouldn't have been surprised to see Jeannie in her favorite place in the window seat of her bedroom. But the house looked vacant.

Matt began walking up the driveway. It hadn't been shoveled. Ribbons of hard-packed snow made by car tires crisscrossed up and down the length of it. Silently they walked to the back door. Matt tried to open it. It was locked.

"Let's try the front door," he said. They walked around to the front. It was locked. "Locked out of my own house," Matt muttered darkly. He sat down on the steps.

"Didn't your mother ever hide a key someplace in case somebody was locked out?" Jamie asked.

"Ya," Matt said, getting up. "It's around in the back."

They retraced their steps. "It's under the mat for the back door," Matt said. "My mother said it was so obvious that no one would think of looking there."

But the doormat was gone. "I guess we'll have to break in," Matt said.

Before Jamie could stop him, Matt picked up a fist-sized rock from under the bushes by the door, walked up to a basement window and chucked the rock at the window. Glass shattered.

Matt slipped into the tiny window well and tapped out

the jagged pieces that were left with his shoe. "Come on, Jamie, we haven't got all day," he said, looking up.

"Be careful of the glass," Jamie said. He began to shiver, fear mixing with the cold.

"There's a table against the wall under the window," Matt said, sticking his feet into the hole. He scooched himself down. "Ya, it's here," he said, looking up. "Come on."

Jamie crawled into the window well and was soon standing on a table in the dark basement of Matt's house. Glass crunched under his feet. "I'll go turn on a light," Matt said, feeling his way to the edge of the table. He hopped down and Jamie heard his footsteps across the floor. The lights flashed on and Jamie saw Matt standing by the stairs, smiling and covered with splotches of mud. He looked down at his own splotches.

"Damn," Jamie said. "The window well didn't look muddy. What will my mom say?"

"We can change into some of my clothes," said Matt. "She won't know the difference. Come on. Let's go upstairs."

The house smelled musty. And it was cold inside. Matt flipped on lights for every room they came into — the kitchen, the dining room, the living room. The living room was filled with cardboard boxes, tops open, crumpled paper sticking out.

Jamie shivered as they walked up the stairs to the bedrooms. He could see Matt's breath.

Matt flipped on the light to his room. "Sheesh! What a mess!" He walked up to the dresser. "What kind of shirt do you want to wear?" They quickly changed into clean clothes.

"Let's go now, Matt," Jamie said. "Somebody's going to see the lights and wonder what's going on."

"Not until I've had a look around," Matt said. "This is my house, after all." He walked out of the room and into the hall. Jamie turned off the light as he followed Matt into Jeannie's room.

Matt walked right up to Jeannie's bed and, kneeling, he reached under the mattress. "It's here," he mumbled. He pulled out a book with a clasp. The clasp was locked. "Damn," he said. With a tug, he ripped the clasp and began flipping through the pages.

"Look at this," Matt said, scanning the page. "July thirtieth. That's her birthday." He read down the page. " 'Got a cute pen from Matt,' " he read aloud, " 'that writes in three colors.' " Matt looked up, smiling. "Look at this," he said, pointing. "She wrote each word in a different color."

Jamie walked over to look.

"You know," Matt said, putting the diary down before Jamie was close enough to see, "when Jeannie and I were real small my mom said that Jeannie could never understand why my birthday always came first after Christmas even though she was older." He lifted up the book again. "Let's see what she said about my birthday." He leafed back through the pages. "Here, June thirteen." He looked down and read aloud. " 'This has been a horrible day. Matt was such a brat all day, but Mom said I had to be nice to him because it was his birthday. Sometimes I wish he'd never been born.' " Matt paused. "That's a pretty rotten thing to say," he said. He continued reading. " 'I gave him a book, which he's probably too dumb to read. I should have gotten him a muzzle.' "

Jamie chuckled. He jammed his hands into his pants pockets. "Let's go, Matt," he said. "It's cold."

"No," Matt said. "Let's go downstairs. I'd like to see what's in the boxes in the living room. If you're cold, we can start a fire in the fireplace." Matt put the diary in his coat pocket. "Jeannie will just die when she finds out I have her diary," he said. It wouldn't take much for her to die, he thought, picturing Jeannie in the hospital bed.

Jamie had to go to the bathroom. When he was done he made sure every light was off upstairs before he came downstairs. As he came down the stairs he saw Matt lighting a huge wad of crumpled newspapers that he had packed into the fireplace. Flames were shooting up the chimney and smoke was billowing out. The living room was filling with smoke, making it difficult to see.

"Help!" Matt yelled, frantically poking at the fire with a newspaper that was folded over. Its tip began to burn. "I forgot to open the flue!"

Jamie rushed to the nearest window and frantically fumbled with the latch. He got it and threw the window open. He rushed to the kitchen and turned on the stove fan. He unlocked the door, propped open the storm door, and then waved the kitchen door back and forth, trying to fan the smoky air out.

A few minutes later Matt came staggering into the kitchen. His face was smudged with charcoal and the hair hanging over his forehead was singed. "It's out," he said. At that moment they heard the sirens. They were getting louder. Matt and Jamie looked at each other in panic, too stunned to move.

Thirteen

*F*irst the firemen came. *They seemed to know right* where to go. They clomped through the back door with big black boots. Each fireman wore gear that looked like a gas mask. Several of them were carrying large fire extinguishers.

"Get out of the house!" one shouted as he rushed into the kitchen. He sounded like he was yelling through a tin can. "Wait by the garage." He clomped into the dining room. Matt and Jamie could hear muffled shouts in the living room as the firemen gathered around the fireplace.

Next the policeman came. He was waiting by the garage as they walked out of the house. The red lights of the fire truck and the blue lights of the police car flashed on the white garage door. The rhythms of the flashing lights played with the rhythms of Matt's thumping heart. The result was a complicated, scary beat. Matt closed his eyes to shut out the frenzy. Images of strobing lights flashed on the inside of his eyelids, like an old home movie of the accident. He opened his eyes to banish those images. He looked around.

Next to him Jamie was babbling. His face was as white

as the snow. The flashing lights made him blush crimson in pulses. Between pulses his flushed face drained of color and he looked like a ghost.

"Just give 'em your name, rank, and serial number," he jabbered. "Name, rank, and serial number, that's all." Jamie was shivering and his teeth were chattering. He became silent, but his teeth kept chattering. He looked to Matt like he was still babbling, with the sound turned off.

"All right, boys, over here." The policeman motioned them closer to the garage door with his thumb. "I have a few questions to ask you."

Matt stared at the policeman. "This is my house," he said through clenched teeth.

"I'm not interested in any stories now, pal," the policeman said, reaching into his heavy coat and taking out a pad and pencil. "I just need to get some information. What's your name, sonny?" He looked at Matt.

"This is my house," Matt said again. His nose began to drip. "I tell you, this is my house!"

A fireman stuck his head out the back door and yelled at the policeman. "Looks OK. A lot of smoke. And a broken basement window." He pointed to the window well to the right of the back stairs. "Broken from the outside." He disappeared into the house.

The policeman looked back at Matt. "Listen, sonny, calm down. You can tell me all about it back at the station. Right now, I need your name, your parents' names, your phone number, and your address. That's all."

"My name is Matthew Smythe," Matt said. He watched the policeman scribble on his notepad.

The policeman looked up. "Parents?"

"They're dead," Matt said.

"Listen, kid. Don't make this any tougher than it has to be." The policeman looked grim. "We need to call your parents so they can meet you down at the station."

"My parents are dead!" Matt's voice was getting shrill.

"Officer, it's true. He lives with me," Jamie said. "His mom died a few weeks ago. My parents are adopting him."

The police officer stared at Jamie. "All right, son, give me *your* name and your parents' names. Go ahead and give me a phone number and address while you're at it."

Jamie talked and Matt watched the firemen come out of the house one by one. They had taken off their smoke masks. "Should I lock this?" the last one yelled at the policeman.

"No," the policeman yelled back. "A team's on its way to investigate." Just then another police car drove up into the driveway. A policeman and a policewoman got out and walked up to the garage.

"Sergeant Tieson," the policewoman called to the policeman who was with Jamie and Matt, "we'll talk to the fire crew. Go ahead and get these kids to the station."

"Right," said Sergeant Tieson. "I'll radio in this info. See you in a little bit." He turned to Matt and Jamie. "OK, Matthew and James." He looked from one to the other. "Let's get going. I'd like you two to sit in the back. No talking, understand?" Jamie shook his head so fast it looked like it would fall off. In fact, he was shaking all over. Matt nodded and started toward the first police car.

"How can he do this?" Matt muttered. "This is my house. This is where I grew up." Each step toward the police car punctuated a word. "This! Is! My! House!"

* * *

While Jamie shuddered and shook next to him in the car, Matt sat like a rock. As they drove along, his thoughts returned to a fall day about two years ago. He and Jamie were going on a picnic and had loaded Matt's knapsack with some bread, a can of beans, some cheese, a few sections of the previous Sunday's newspaper, and a box of matches. They also hid some Twinkies and some soda in a side compartment.

The air was brisk and the sky was deep, deep blue. The crisp leaves were ankle-deep as Matt and Jamie walked toward a secluded picnic area in the park behind Jamie's house. Kicking and shuffling through the red and yellow and brown leaves of the maple, ash, and oak trees was like wading through a bowl of cornflakes. The slightly acrid smell of the rotting leaves on the ground always made Matt happy, yet vaguely sad. Sweet and sour, like Chinese food, he thought. Hot and cold like the liquid nitrogen his doctor used to freeze off his warts. Happy, sad — that was fall, when nights grew longer and a fresh new school year became boring routine.

The picnic was fun and relaxed. Matt and Jamie collected some fallen wood and made a fire in the stone hearth with a metal grate spread over it. They heated up the beans. When the beans began bubbling they ate them.

They went on to the second course — toasted cheese sandwiches. The fire had not died down, and flames licked at the bread and burned it before the cheese even got warm.

"Guess we'll just have to eat it raw," Jamie said. He crammed his mouth with a hunk of cheese trapped between chunks of charred bread.

They stuffed themselves as they sat propped up against

two nearby trees. They topped off their meal with Twinkies and soda.

Jamie belched loudly. "What a gas," he said.

Matt stared at the leaves covering the ground and blanketing the hillside. He glanced at the area around the grate that he and Jamie had cleared of leaves.

"Jamie," he said, turning to his friend, "do you think these leaves really burn as fast as people say they do?"

Jamie looked at the leaves thoughtfully. "I don't know. We had a pretty hard time just lighting the paper and getting our fire started."

Matt looked at the leaves on the hillside. "I don't think we could made those leaves burn if we wanted to," he said, pointing to a small pile on the other side of the stone hearth.

"Why don't we find out?" Jamie asked.

"I think those beans are fighting with the cheese sandwich," Matt said, groaning as he struggled to his feet.

"Ya, things are getting pretty loud down there," Jamie said, letting go another powerful belch.

"I think the matches are here." Jamie walked over to the knapsack and reached into the side compartment. He pulled them out. "Tell you what. Let's have a contest to see who can get the leaves burning first."

"OK," Matt said. "Let's set a limit of five matches each, tops."

"OK," Jamie said. He counted out five matches and handed them to Matt. He counted out five more, closed the matchbox and put it on the ground. "Now, how will we light 'em?" he asked.

"Any way you can," Matt said. "Ready, set, go!"

Matt dropped to his knees and pulled back the flap

covering the zipper of his jeans. He struck the match down the length of the zipper. A few small sparks flashed, but the match didn't catch.

Jamie watched Matt and quickly dropped to his knees. "That's clever," he said. "Don't catch your pants on fire."

"Don't worry," Matt said, striking a second match.

"This tickles!" Jamie said, giggling.

"Aha!" Matt's third match burst into flame. He quickly cupped his left hand around it and slowly lowered it to a pile of leaves.

"Aha yourself," Jamie said. His fourth match was burning. But it went out before he could protect it from the breeze. He quickly lit his last match and shielded it in a cupped hand as he reached toward a leaf pile.

Matt was surprised at how quickly the leaves caught fire. He blew gently on the tiny fire and watched, fascinated, as the flames devoured one leaf and then two and then four and on and on.

"Hey, Matt," Jamie said. "You won, but look!" He pointed to his own little fire. "They really burn fast!"

Matt and Jamie watched as the flames spread and the smoke curled up. "I guess we better put them out," Matt said, dreamily. But just then a gust of wind scooted some of the burning leaves a few feet up the hill. Before they knew it, the fire had tripled in size.

"Whoops," Jamie said. He jumped up and began stomping on the burning leaves. Matt scrambled to help. Another gust fanned the flames, which were now shin-high. The fire spread farther up the hill.

"Help!" Matt yelled. "My side is spreading!"

"So's mine," Jamie yelled, frantically stamping away. He

tried to smother the fire by kicking more leaves onto it. The flames jumped higher.

"We can't put this out!" Jamie cried. The smoke and frustration brought tears to his eyes. "Let's get help!"

"I'll stay. You run to get help!" Matt shouted. Jamie grabbed the knapsack and ran up the hill.

Matt kicked and stomped and swore and spat at the spreading fire. Smoke billowed and rolled up the hill. Twigs cracked as they burned. Matt's jeans began to smolder, and heat was building uncomfortably in the soles of his sneakers.

"Goddamn it!" Matt said over and over again. He kept up his wild dance until he heard the scream of the fire engines coming into the park. He walked over to the hearth and sat down. "What will I tell them?" he mumbled.

Firemen galumphed up to the picnic area, carrying fire extinguishers. They ran to the fire, which had spread itself thin and was just beginning to die out. It hissed as they sprayed water on it.

One of the firemen knelt next to Matt. "How'd it start?" he asked.

"I don't know," Matt replied, looking up. He swallowed hard and hoped Jamie hadn't told them anything. "My friend and I were walking by and we saw it burning and we tried to put it out." The fireman got out a pad and pencil and began scribbling. "We couldn't, so he ran to get help."

The fireman studied him. "I'll need your name and your friend's name," he said. He paused. "Thanks for helping us out." He didn't sound like he meant it.

*   *   *

137

At the police station, Matt and Jamie were marched into an office and Sergeant Tieson questioned them some more. He asked about birthdates, parents, schools, and when he was finished he sat back, as if catching his breath and clearing his mind. He stared at them.

"OK, now, tell me what happened."

The story gushed from Jamie. Sergeant Tieson interrupted Jamie every once in a while to ask Matt if he agreed with what Jamie was saying. Each time Matt nodded his head and said "yes." When Jamie was finished, he sat, tired and limp, as if getting the story out had literally drained him.

"Do you know how dangerous that was?" Sergeant Tieson asked.

Matt and Jamie nodded. "Now I'm taking your word about the story — until all the facts are in. If your story is true, at the very least you did something both stupid and wrong," he scolded. "You two are old enough to know right from wrong, and if you don't, it's high time you learned."

"I was in my own house," Matt said.

"That may be true," the sergeant said. "But breaking into any house is bad news. And starting big bonfires in the living room is really bad news."

Another policeman knocked on the door and stuck his head in. "The Fletchers are out here."

"Wait here," Sergeant Tieson said. "I'll be back in a moment."

"Oh boy," Jamie shuddered. "What will Dad say? Ohboyohboyohboyohboy."

Just then the door opened and Scott and Judy rushed in, followed by Sergeant Tieson.

"Jamie!" Judy cried. She turned to Matt. "Matt! I'm *furious* with you both . . . and I'm so glad you're all right!"

Scott stood by quietly. Jamie stood up and Judy reached out and drew him to her. Jamie began sobbing into her coat. Matt looked up from where he was sitting, feeling confused, as if he had an itch but didn't know where. He wanted to cry but he didn't want to cry. He wanted to explain but he didn't want to explain. He wanted to hug Judy but he didn't want to hug Judy. What he really wanted to do was hug his mother. He needed her! And she wasn't there.

Matt buried his face in his hands and closed his eyes tightly. "Momma, Momma, Momma," he blubbered. Nobody heard his muffled cry. Scott came over and sat down next to Matt and put his arm around Matt's shoulder.

When everybody calmed down, Scott got up and walked over to Sergeant Tieson. "Is everything taken care of?" he asked.

"Yes, you have custody of the boys. We'll be calling in a day or so to confirm the story the boys gave us."

Driving home, Scott said, quietly, "I never thought I'd be picking up any child of mine from the police station." He drove on for a moment. "You may be interested to know that you were reported by a neighbor who thought the house was being burglarized. When she saw the smoke she called the fire department." He sounded grim. "That was a very stupid thing you two did. You did something that could have ended in disaster. And it hurts to think you would do something like that behind our backs. You were supposed to be at a movie, for Chrissake!"

Matt opened his mouth to speak. No sound came out. The silence grew heavy.

Scott cleared his throat. "We're lucky that nothing was hurt — except all of our prides. And" — he turned to Judy — "swallowing a little pride every day can be as good for you as taking vitamins. But that doesn't make what you did right. I want you both to understand how serious that was." His voice had regained its sharp edge. "You're both grounded for the rest of the month. And you better not burn *our* house down!"

That's an unfair thing to say, Matt thought.

Scott turned off the main road and onto a residential street.

"Is anybody hungry?" Judy asked quietly.

"Ya," Jamie said haltingly. "Being arrested sure makes a guy hungry." He laughed nervously.

Scott's face melted slowly and a smile twitched at the corners of his mouth. He began to chuckle. The air in the car seemed easier to breathe.

"I love chicken lips and pig feet," Matt said quietly.

Judy smiled. "Would you settle for lasagna?"

Fourteen

T he winter storm began as Matt and Jamie were going to bed. Snow materialized magically from the black sky. "Heavenly dandruff on the shoulder of earth," his mother used to call it. Maybe some of it was her dandruff, Matt thought.

But the flakes looked too heavy. As Matt watched from the bedroom window, he expected the snowflakes to splat as they hit the sidewalk. Instead, they delicately disappeared as if they had gone right through the cement and penetrated deep into the earth.

On the lawn, however, Matt watched the snow slowly accumulate, bleaching the dirty grays and tans of the grass. The bushes turned ghostlike, and Matt remembered the night of the accident and the ghostly cars parked along the street.

The weatherman on the television news said that it was going to be the biggest storm of the year.

"A blizzard!" Jamie chattered excitedly as they got ready for bed. "Sounds like a cross between a lizard and a buzzard."

"Ya." Matt tried to picture what such a creature would look like.

Jamie was in high spirits. He threw his socks at Matt. "These smell as bad as your breath," he said.

Matt picked them up with his thumb and forefinger and held them at arm's length. "How many days have you worn these?" he asked, screwing up his face in disgust.

"Seven," Jamie answered. "A new record, I might add. Think I should try for eight?"

"If you put these on again, your toes will shrivel up and fall off," Matt said, dumping the socks on a pile of Jamie's other clothes.

Matt felt snug under the covers. He thought of the snow covering the world like a soft blanket. From inside a house, snow always looked warm and inviting. He pictured his mother lying on her back covered with a blanket of snow. Matt wiggled his toes. It may look cozy on top, Matt thought. But it's not the kind of blanket you can tuck in around your feet.

Soon he fell asleep. And he began to dream.

What wonderful smells! Matt breathed the air in deeply as he walked down the forest path. The smells of musty leaves and damp earth were strong — like the smell of a wet, mud-splattered dog. He breathed out slowly, his breath fogging as it hit the cold air. Matt jammed his hands farther into the pockets of his shorts, threw his head back, and laughed at the sky.

It's great to be alive! Matt laughed again and shook his head, feeling hair brush against the back of his neck. The world glowed and Matt saw delightful surprises everywhere he looked. Snow on logs and branches looked like blobs of whipped cream and made wonderful shapes — a long-nosed gnome's face here, rabbit ears over there, a bent elbow escaping behind a tree to his right.

The path felt wonderful under Matt's bare feet. The fluffy snow was cold, but his feet felt warm. Matt puckered his lips to whistle, but no sound came out of his dry lips.

Never mind, Matt thought. I should have brought a hat. And he kicked some snow with his foot, twirled on his other foot, and walked backward in the same direction he'd been going.

The bare branches of the trees looked like ink lines scribbled on the cloudy sky. In the distance Matt saw darker clouds looming. A gust of wind rattled through the forest and snatched a lone leaf that clung to the tip of a branch overhead and whisked it by Matt's head. Snow, as fine and hard as sand, began to hit him in the face. Matt closed his eyes, turned his back to the coming storm, and kept walking.

Matt wasn't cold. But the wind sounded cold, and that made him shiver. The gusts became stronger and the snow granules stung as they hit the back of his neck and arms and legs. Good thing I wore a shirt, Matt thought, and he turned the collar up.

Darkness descended and the snow flew at Matt with more intensity. The flakes were larger and softer, though, and Matt could feel the snow gathering like a cap on the crown of his head. It melted, forming trickles of water that tickled down his neck and behind his ears.

A rabbit leaped across the path in front of Matt, ears back, as if pursued. Matt stopped and cocked his head in the direction from which the rabbit had come. He couldn't hear the crashing of a larger animal through the forest underbrush. Instead he heard the approaching, growing howl of the wind. It sounded like a pack of wolves — coming right at him. A gust smacked Matt with such violence that it almost knocked him over.

This is becoming quite a storm, Matt thought. This is fun.

The temperature plunged and snow began to fly by so furiously Matt could barely see his feet. I really should have worn shoes, Matt thought as he started walking. But then, the shoes would have gotten wet and cold.

The wind became colder and colder. But Matt felt warmer and warmer. A warmth, like the glow of embers, came from inside his body. The wind seemed to fan these embers. The harder the wind blew the more toasty Matt felt.

The snow drifted over the trail. Matt stepped into piles of snow, deep as his knees. The snow came in blinding gusts. The wind howled and shrieked. Matt bent forward, letting the wind slip over his shoulder and bowed head. He stared at the path ahead. The storm was losing its playfulness. This isn't fun anymore, Matt thought. Maybe it's time to go home. He picked up his pace.

In the middle of the path, a few feet in front of him, Matt saw a robin. Its feathers were puffed up and its eyes half-closed against the driving snow. Matt stopped in his tracks and stared at the bird. The robin didn't move. It only closed its eyes and puffed out its feathers even more, shaking off some of the settled snow. Only the top of its red breast peeked out above the snow.

Matt stepped closer, moving slowly and carefully so that

he wouldn't frighten the bird. The robin didn't budge. Matt took another step. Still it didn't move. Matt stared as the robin closed its eyes tighter and opened its mouth a crack. It looked like it was panting.

Matt reached out and touched the bird very gently on its head. The robin's eyes flew open and its mouth gaped, but still it didn't move. It glared at Matt with half-closed eyes.

Matt stroked the soft feathers behind its neck and on its back. With a look of resentment, the robin refluffed its feathers and tried to hop away from Matt's hand. Instead, it toppled beak-first into the snow.

Quickly, Matt reached under the bird and lifted it out of the snow. Its cold feet dug into his palm as it tried to anchor itself and keep from tipping over. The robin's eyes were open now and staring at Matt's face. Matt saw no fear in those eyes, only weariness. But as Matt watched, the eyes glazed over. Matt felt shivers that were invisible under the puffy feathers. With each ripple, the robin tightened its grip in Matt's palm.

This bird's freezing to death, Matt thought. Quickly, but careful not to jostle the bird, Matt peeled his shirt off his left arm and over his head. He brought the shirt down his right arm to his hand and gently wrapped it around the bird. He drew the bundle to his chest and cradled it in his left arm. Matt trotted down the path.

I've got to save this bird, he thought. I've got to save this bird. Matt searched his mind for the nearest warm place where he could revive the bird. The wind whipped at his bare back and snow fell into the back of his shorts and melted.

145

Matt trotted as smoothly as he could. Do birds get motion sick? he wondered. Matt was afraid to check for fear of letting cold air in through the folds of the shirt.

The church, Matt thought. The church near the forest path. That would be a good place to warm the bird. Matt hunched his shoulders and picked up his pace. Don't die, little bird, he whispered. Don't die. The grip of the bird's feet grew weaker. Perhaps the bird is getting warm, Matt thought. It is shivering less. Matt plowed through a snow drift that came almost over his shorts.

But maybe the bird is dying, losing its strength and its grip on my hand, Matt thought. Matt slid to a stop and, sheltering the bird against the wind, he unwrapped his shirt just enough to peek at the robin.

Matt saw that the bird was on its side. Its legs were twitching and its eyes were closed. He could barely see the robin breathe. Horror-struck, Matt covered up the bird and charged ahead.

Matt burst into a meadow. The wind swirled around him. The silhouette of the church was barely visible in the raging snow. He ran toward the looming church. He scrambled up the stairs to the huge front doors. Matt reached out his left hand and yanked at one door and then the other. They were both locked. In his frustration, Matt kicked at the doors. Pain shot through his bare foot.

Why would anyone lock up a church? Matt asked himself frantically. The answer echoed in his head. Matt recognized his own voice. "Goddamn Him to hell! Goddamn Him to hell!"

"I didn't mean it!" Matt yelled at the doors. Tears of frustration streamed down his face, freezing on his cheeks in crinkly streaks. "I didn't mean it! Let me in!" He kicked the door again, and through the pain he heard a booming voice rumble hollowly through the church. "Our Father, who aren't in heaven, Hollow is thy game...." And then laughter, big booming laughter. The shrill of the wind grew louder and more piercing, drowning out the laughter. Terrified, Matt turned and blindly scurried down the steps. "I've got to get home," he muttered. Tears fell in frozen beads as they came from his eyes.

The bird flopped around in the shirt. It was losing its warmth. Matt's hand began to chill as the robin chilled. The robin grew heavier and harder, like a lump of feathered ice, and a bone-deep cold moved slowly up his arm.

Sing, bird, sing! Sing, dead bird, sing!

The snow crunched under his bare feet to the rhythm of his chant. The cold moved into his shoulder.

Matt stumbled and sprawled, landing on his elbows to protect the bundled bird, hitting the cement steps of a house. Matt looked up. It was his house. And a light was on in his mother's bedroom! Quickly he scrambled to his feet and, reaching out his trembling hand to the door, he grabbed the knob and turned. It didn't budge. The cold in his other arm moved into his neck. Quickly Matt reached for the doorbell. He punched it over and over and over again. Ring! Ring! Ring! Ring!

Matt sat bolt upright in bed, panting and sweating. In the pitch dark he heard his heart pounding. The phone was ringing. It stopped and Matt heard the muffled sound of a tired voice. He shivered, remembering his dream. His entire right arm was completely asleep. Suddenly it all made sense.

A minute passed. And then another. A light snapped on in the hallway. Matt heard someone shuffling down the hall. The steps came to the door and Matt watched calmly as Scott walked toward the bed. Scott stopped and looked up into Matt's face.

"Matt," Scott said quietly.

"I know," Matt said. "Jeannie's dead."

"Yes." Scott reached up and took Matt's hand. "I'm sorry."

"I'm not," Matt said softly. "It's hard to make a dead bird sing." Tears began to well up in his eyes. "And it hurts to cry frozen tears."

Scott looked puzzled. But Matt didn't care. His arm prickled with pins and needles as it slowly came back to life.

Fifteen

eannie's funeral was short and sweet. For Matt, it was almost happy.

His sister had been fairly popular in school. Even though the funeral was on a Tuesday, students were allowed to attend. Jeannie's classmates stuck together off to the side. Before the service, Matt watched them as they made self-conscious conversation and stole glances at each other. Matt thought they were like a herd of sheep — all afraid they would be nabbed like Jeannie if they strayed from the flock.

In the front of the flock, looking stricken, was Ralph. Ralph hadn't talked to Matt since their walk. But Matt found himself walking toward the Porter house often after school. He and Jamie even collected litter — cans mostly — along the way and then tossed them into the Porter front yard. And Matt sometimes fantasized about burning the Porter house down or throwing rocks in Porter's window or spray-painting obscenities on his driveway and sidewalk.

In fact, somebody already had decorated Mr. Porter's car and driveway with spray paint. Matt read one evening in the newspaper about a marked increase in vandalism in the area where Mr. Porter lived. The article said: "This vandalism, attributed to high school students, is focused on the house of a resident the police will not name. 'We've seen everything from broken windows to spray-painted slogans on the sidewalk,' said a police spokesman."

Matt looked around some more. Some of Jeannie's teachers were there, too, clumped together like the students. Each teacher looked nice enough. But as a group, they were kind of scary. Maybe they're protecting each other from people who ask questions they can't answer, Matt thought.

Why did Jeannie die, anyway? Mr. Untterbach was trying his hardest to answer that question. Matt listened a moment. The pastor wasn't hitting on all cylinders — he was spinning his wheels and not going anywhere. Matt let his thoughts wander.

Jeannie died because she wouldn't have been Jeannie if she'd lived, Matt thought. Her brain was damaged. She might not have been able to talk or read. Her legs were gone, her face was smashed. Her mother was dead.

"Mother and daughter are together now in heaven," Mr. Untterbach said. He sounded a million miles away. Bullshit, Matt thought. But secretly he hoped that they were.

Matt had read a part of Jeannie's diary every day since he'd taken it from under her bed. He remembered a section of it now. She'd had a big fight with their mother about a swimsuit she wanted to buy. Their mother thought it was scandalous. The fight had been pretty vicious. At the time, Matt wondered if they'd ever speak to each other again.

Little did he know. That night Jeannie wrote: "Had a big fight with the bitch-witch. I'm exhausted. It's getting harder and harder to get what I want. It's kind of funny. I don't even like the swimsuit that much. I'd feel silly with half of my boobs and butt hanging out. I'd probably never wear it. I just wish that Mom trusted me enough to know I'd never buy it even if she said I could."

Matt smiled. It was funny. And it was sad. Now that Jeannie was gone, he knew her better than when she was alive. And he not only knew her better, he even liked her. He remembered one day when she wrote: "Matt is growing up. He'll probably be pretty good looking too." And this was the same person who used to call him "Door Matt, the Matador"!

Matt was so absorbed in his thoughts that he didn't even know when the service was over.

"Matt, we should leave for the cemetery," Judy said quietly, taking his hand.

He and Jamie and Judy and Scott went outside to another limousine, which followed another hearse with another body in it. Matt felt as if he was reenacting a vivid dream.

At the cemetery happy thoughts wandered into and out of Matt's head during the burial service. He was surprised that his thoughts were so happy — but he was also relieved.

He remembered a time when he and Jeannie were very young and taking a bath together. Their mother left them to play in the water and Jeannie stood up to look out the window which was right above the tub.

"I dare you to run over to Mrs. Hutchin's house and ring her doorbell," she said.

"Oh, ya?" Matt answered.

"I double-dare you."

"What do I get?" Matt asked.

"A nickel," Jeannie replied.

"OK," Matt said, climbing out of the tub, water streaming off him.

"But you have to do it naked," Jeannie said, smiling from ear to ear.

Matt grabbed his shorts and scooted out the door. He put them on at the top of the stairs and scurried down, through the living room, out the door and into the glorious spring day. He barely missed being hit by a car. He ran up to the Hutchins' front door, rang the bell, and skedaddled back home, up the stairs, and stopped, breathlessly, in front of the tub. He began to take off his shorts.

"No fair!" Jeannie sputtered. Matt knew that she'd been watching from the window. "You weren't naked!"

"Oh yes I was," Matt said. "See?" He pulled off his shorts and pointed downward. "I was naked under my shorts!" And he climbed into the tub.

Jeannie was being buried very close to their parents. Matt glanced over at the snow-covered mound that marked his mother's grave. Matt wondered if the blank date under her name on the stone had been changed.

I don't know if I want to be buried when I die, Matt thought. Matt had read someplace that hair and fingernails and toenails kept growing after people died. He didn't know if it was true or not. But it gave him the creeps to think about dead men in their caskets with scruffy beards and dead women with long toenails mashed against the front of their shoes. I'd rather be cremated, Matt thought, and have my ashes scattered someplace. Where? I'll have to think about that, he decided.

As he thought, his gaze drifted upward to the blue sky. A couple of birds that looked like hawks soared high above the field next to the cemetery. Looking for rabbits and mice, he thought.

Out of the corner of his eyes, he saw a bird flit from one tree alongside the field to another tree. Matt turned his head and watched as the bird flew to a tree in the cemetery. Matt gasped. It was a robin!

It's not spring, Matt thought. Robins don't come back at this time of the year. The bird ruffled its feathers and began to sing.

Sing, dead bird. Sing!

It was a robin! Matt stared. And his heart did cartwheels in his chest.

Sing, dead bird. Sing!

Matt smiled and looked down at Jeannie's casket, poised above the rectangular hole in front of him.

The service ended and Matt waited a few moments before standing up. Scott, Judy, and Jamie slowly followed the collection of people meandering back to their cars. They were talking to Jeannie's English teacher. Jeannie had been very fond of him. Matt was still lost in thought and straggling behind.

Out of the corner of his left eye, Matt saw someone move

from behind a large oak tree. Startled, Matt turned toward the tree. In case of trouble, he glanced up the hill to see where Scott, Judy, and Jamie were.

Matt took a step backward and a man stepped out from behind the tree, a rumpled hat in his hands. Matt recognized him instantly and froze. He wanted to scream, but a tightness clutched at his throat so hard that he could barely breathe.

"I, um," the man stammered, thickly. "I, um, I'm Frank Porter, the, um, the guy who, um, ran into you, you know, um, during the, the, um, accident."

The man's eyes were bloodshot and his hands trembled slightly. The tremor of his voice was at once disarming and infuriating.

"I, um, I just wanted to tell you, um, that, I, ah, um ..." The trembling of his hands grew more violent and his knuckles whitened as he grabbed more tightly onto his hat. His mouth contorted and he lost all control of his face. "I'm sorry," he blurted. "I can't tell you how sorry I am." Huge tears streamed down his face, spreading into the tiny crinkles in the flabby folds of skin on his face. The man began to sob.

Matt watched the man's agony and his heart pounded, pounded, pounded, louder, louder, louder.

"Hey, Matt," Scott called. "Come on.... Oh my God! Porter, stay away from that boy or I'll call the police!" Scott and Jeannie's teacher came running toward them. "Matt," Scott gasped, running up beside Matt and putting his arm around him. "Are you all right?" Scott hadn't taken his eyes off Mr. Porter for an instant.

"Yes," Matt whispered hoarsely. "I hate this son of a

bitch!" he hissed through clenched teeth, staring at the sobbing man. The man was shaking uncontrollably and looked so limp that Matt didn't know what was holding him upright.

"Porter," Scott said, "you better go. This certainly isn't helping anybody. You're drunk as a skunk!" Scott's voice was hard, almost cruel.

"Look," Mr. Porter gasped. "I just wanted . . . to say . . . I'm sorry." He began to stumble off toward the cars. He stopped and looked back at Matt. "And leave my house alone!" He pointed a wagging finger at Matt, turned and continued stumbling toward the cars.

"I hate you!" Matt screamed behind him, his fists clenched so tightly that his fingers hurt. "I hope your house burns to the ground — with you in it!" Several people who had not quite reached their cars started coming back, wondering what the fuss was about.

Matt fought his tears. Even though he had wanted to, he didn't feel any better now that he'd screamed at the man who'd killed his mother and sister. In fact, he felt rotten. He felt as if he'd kicked a puppy in the head. At the same time, he wanted to yell something worse. But he couldn't think of anything worse.

His anger was confused by a feeling of pity. He didn't want to feel sorry for the drunk! Anger at himself piled onto anger at Mr. Porter — touching off a blinding explosion of anger. Matt leaped toward Mr. Porter, fists swinging. He beat on the man's back as hard as he could. Startled, Mr. Porter turned to look, stumbled, and fell sprawling to the ground. Matt began to kick. He was just about to kick the quivering, flabby, wide-eyed face when Jeannie's teacher grabbed Matt by the shoulders and pulled him back.

"Matt!" the teacher said, restraining him. "Matt! Calm down!"

Several men ran up and helped Mr. Porter to his feet. He had dried leaves and grass stuck to his coat and mud on his elbows. He stared at Matt in terror. Throughout the episode he'd never let go the grip on his hat.

Matt struggled to escape. His legs buckled and he sagged, his knees scraping the ground. He regained his footing and he gasped for air. Matt spat on the ground at Mr. Porter's feet. His eyes narrowed. "My mom's dead. My sister's dead. And you should be dead. But you're not." His throat tightened. "And now you have to live with yourself. I feel sorry for you!"

"Matt, let's go," Scott said. Drained of energy, Matt stumbled alongside Scott toward Jamie and Judy. Scott called to the teacher, who was still breathing hard and standing nearby. "Henry, if Porter drove here, call the police. His license was suspended until the trial. We're leaving."

That evening, Scott called Matt into his den. He closed the door and motioned for Matt to sit on the big leather chair. Scott sat facing Matt on the leather footstool. He cleared his throat.

"Matt," he said, clasping his hands in front of him and resting his elbows on his knees, "I just want to say something about this morning and Frank Porter. I'm not going to lecture you. I just want you to think about some things." He cleared his throat again. "Frank Porter is a very sick man. He's an alcoholic. He needs help. And hopefully he'll get it before he kills anyone else or" — Scott looked right at Matt — "or himself."

"I hope he does," Matt said, sullenly.

"You have every reason to hate him, Matt. He did an unspeakably terrible thing. He killed your mother and Jeannie the same as if he'd shot them with a gun or stabbed them with a knife." He paused. "But, Matt, hatred is an awful thing to carry around. Don't let it control you. It's powerful and it will control you if you let it."

"I thought you weren't going to lecture me," Matt said, looking up. Whose side was Scott on, anyway?

Scott looked down at his hands. "You're right. Let me tell you a story," he said. "Not too long ago, there was a boy about your age who lived next to a big, beautiful Saint Bernard. The boy had a baseball mitt that he loved dearly. In fact, he'd saved nickels from his lunch money to buy it, and every afternoon when his stomach growled and ached from not having lunch he'd think about that baseball mitt he was going to buy with the nickel he'd saved that day.

"Well, the boy finally got the mitt, and that must have been the happiest day of his life. He rubbed the mitt with oil, he practiced catch with the high school kid down the block, he wore it everywhere — sometimes even when he was biking. He kept it by his chair at dinner, kept it by his desk at school, and, if the truth were known, he slept with it — just like a little kid with a teddy bear." Scott looked up. His mouth drooped into a sad smile.

"But one day, the boy left the mitt on the back steps of his house — for a whole afternoon. And when he came back to get it, he saw the neighbor's Saint Bernard chewing on it. Most of the thumb was gone, and the webbing was shredded and the dog was happily gnawing on several other fingers. The boy threw a rock at the dog, who dropped the glove and lumbered away. But the boy vowed to get even with the dog. He even dreamed of cutting its ears off and cutting off its tail and making the dog chew on them, he hated it so much. Every chance he got, he tormented the dog next door.

"One day, the boy saw the dog chewing on a big hip joint that their neighbor had brought back from the grocery store. The boy was so overcome with hatred, seeing the dog enjoying himself so much, that he ran up and grabbed the bone and began to beat the dog on the head with it.

"Being a dog, the dog leaped up, snarling, and chomped onto the boy's hands and arms and started shaking them." Scott looked at his hands again. Slowly, he held them out for Matt to see.

"Look. Have you ever seen these scars before?" He pointed to one that ran up the back of his right hand, over his wrist, and halfway up to his elbow. They were faint but ragged. "That's what the dog did to the boy." Matt stared and looked up at Scott. "There are more on this hand," he said, holding out his left hand. "It took five operations before I could use all of my fingers — and my little finger still isn't quite right." He bent the little finger on his right hand slightly. "That's all the farther it goes." Scott put his hands back down.

"It was painful. It hurt. And I hated the dog more than ever. But you know what? I hated myself even more for feeling that way when the neighbors were ordered to put the dog to sleep. They killed the dog because of my stupid, hotheaded mistake. And they bought me a new mitt. But it took me a long time before I could bring myself to use it." Scott paused.

"Hatred's a horrible feeling to carry around. But I don't want to lecture."

Matt looked at his feet. His hatred for Mr. Porter did make him feel dirty. Unwashed and smelly. In the head.

"Don't let hatred control you. It always seems to hurt everybody, especially the person who is doing the hating."

Scott stood up. "Sorry I got carried away. But I'd like you to think about these things."

Before Scott got to the door Matt looked up. "Scott?"

Scott stopped and turned around. "Yes."

"Can you hate someone and feel sorry for them at the same time?" Matt's head was bowed and his shoulders sagged.

Scott walked over to him, sat on the arm of the chair and put his arm around Matt. "Yes, I think so," Scott said.

"I hate Mr. Porter," Matt said. "And I feel sorry for him. Then I hate myself for feeling sorry for him and hate him even more for making me miserable and . . . and . . ."

"And confused?" Scott asked quietly.

"Ya." Matt looked up. Tears came to his eyes. "How should I feel? I want to kick his face in, but I know he didn't mean to kill anybody. I hate him for killing Mom and Jeannie, but I feel sorry for him. How should I feel?" Tears spilled over and dropped onto his lap.

Scott pulled him closer. "It hurts, doesn't it? And it's confusing. Matt, it sounds silly, but you'll figure it out. It takes time. You never forget the hurt and the pain, but

159

you learn to understand it and live with it." He ruffled Matt's hair. "Matt, we have faith in you. And we'll help every way we can."

Matt sniffed and nodded his head. *Will the hurt ever go away? Will I ever feel normal again?*

"Hey Matt," Jamie said as they were getting ready for bed that night. "Let me quiz you on our Spanish." Their class had spent the past week learning the Spanish words for different parts of the body. They were going to have a test on Friday.

"What's this?" Jamie pointed to his head.

"*La cabeza,*" Matt answered.

"Good. What's this!" Jamie pointed to one of his feet.

"*El pie,*" Matt answered.

"Right again. What's this?" Jamie pointed to his nose.

"*La nariz,*" Matt answered. "Hey, I've got one for you. What's this?" Matt pointed to his elbow.

Jamie thought for a minute as he sat on his bed and took off his socks. "I don't think we had that one, Matt," he said.

"You should know it anyway," Matt said. "El bow!" He laughed. "Get it? EL BOW!"

Jamie grinned. "Home of the funnybone," he said.

At times like these, Matt couldn't imagine not having a brother. Sometimes he even felt guilty that he felt so good about being in Jamie's family. It wouldn't have happened if his mother was still alive.

"*Buenos* nachos, you dip," Matt said, crawling into bed.

Jamie laughed and turned out the light. "Goodnight, *hermano.*"

Sixteen

The gentle spring air puffed through the open window and washed over Matt's body in delicate waves. Matt couldn't sleep. The night was clear, the stars were bright, and the moon was full. It was well past midnight, and Matt just couldn't close his eyes.

He felt restless, like a dog during a full moon, full of vague roaming thoughts. Matt could hear the soft, regular breathing of Jamie below him. Sometimes hearing Jamie's breathing made Matt sleepy, like the sound of a stream burbling or waves lapping on a beach. But tonight it was keeping Matt awake.

The darkness was soft, like slightly tarnished silverware. Sounds seemed louder to Matt and smells seemed stronger.

Matt could hear no cars, no voices, no slamming doors. This made the sleepy chirps of an occasional bird and the bolder sound of crickets as clear as the stars in the sky. Every once in a while, Matt heard fainter rustlings in last year's dried leaves that were under the bushes next to the house. He imagined a cat stalking a mouse. He pictured a toad, stiff from the night chill, bouncing along the house like a half-filled water balloon. Matt cringed at the possibility that his imagination would burst the toad on a sharp rock or stick, leaving a puddle of toad juice next to a scrap of shrunken toad skin. But his imagination was kinder, shifting its attention to the smells around him.

The room smelled a little musty — a combination of the sour breath that takes over when the toothpaste breath wears thin, dirty clothes piled on the floor, dust mixed with an occasional breath of fresh air from the window. Scott had fixed his famous south-of-the-border beans for dinner that night. He used fresh-frozen green chilis that a friend of his from law school sometimes sent from New Mexico. After dinner, Jamie referred to their bedroom only as "the gas chamber." Jamie knew what he was talking about. Both Matt and Jamie had been farting all night. Matt heard a gentle rumble and hiss down below and waited for the smell to waft up to him.

But before it did, a puff of air came from the window, carrying on it the wonderful spring freshness — the smell of moist earth that reminded him of mushrooms. His nose glowed and his nostrils widened.

Matt filled his lungs with the sweet air and held his breath. Carefully and quietly he climbed down from his bed. He walked toward the window and stuck his head outside. Breathing deeply now, he looked out at the peaceful trees with their delicate new leaves, barely open. He looked down at the grass, tufts of thick, high grass in patches on the uncut lawn where the neighbor's dog pooped. The crocuses by the large oak tree outside his window were closed up for the night and the heads of the daffodils by the driveway faintly bobbed in the breeze.

Matt felt drawn to the outside. He turned and walked out of the bedroom, down the stairs, through the kitchen, and outside. Matt planted his feet firmly apart, looked straight up at the stars, and let the breeze and the moonlight bathe the length of his pale white body. He hugged himself and swayed back and forth. He realized for the first time that he was naked as the day he was born — and outside!

He couldn't have cared less. The damp grass of the backyard felt wonderful between his toes, and he started toward the woods, aimed right at the path that led through the forest. The moon shone brightly, making his pale skin glow from his toes to his head. Matt paused, held out his hand and looked at it. The skin looked like polished ivory — smooth and soft. He moved his fingers, and they seemed like someone else's.

He turned to look at his rear end. It was the whitest part of him. From this angle, his rear looked like a half-moon. He was mooning the moon! Matt smiled.

He had never hiked in the woods without clothes before. If somebody had ever suggested it to Matt, he would have laughed and made fun of the idea. It was silly. As much as he enjoyed being naked at home, being naked in public had always embarrassed Matt. It made him feel too exposed, vulnerable to ridicule or pranks. At almost every swim meet, a few of the older boys took somebody's clothes and towel from the locker room and tossed them into the hall or even outside. Nobody ever helped the hapless victim, because that always meant they would be next. So the poor boy would have to cover up what he could with his hands, scurry out and grab what he could. If he was lucky, he grabbed pants, which meant he wouldn't have to make a second embarrassing dash.

Sometimes, if it was a coed meet, one of the older boys would invite the girls to watch the spectacle. Luckily that had never happened to Matt. Although he laughed along with the rest, Matt never quite understood what was so funny. To him the human body was beautiful, not comical.

But being naked tonight, with the stars overhead and the moon shining bright, seemed completely natural — like being at home. In fact, he soon forgot his nakedness altogether. Several times, as he strutted along, he tried to put his hands in pants pockets, only to find he didn't have any pants on.

Matt was alone but he didn't feel alone. He felt watched. Normally, at night, in the woods, that feeling would have caused him to look for monsters lurking in the shadows or animals on the prowl.

But Matt felt the watching eyes were friendly, quiet, gentle, nice. For a moment, the smells in the forest mixed and Matt's nose tingled with the fragrance of — of his mother's perfume! Impossible. Yet he felt, suddenly, her closeness, her gaze . . . her love. Matt took a deep breath and looked at the Milky Way, which stretched overhead, dim only where it was outshone by the moon. If the moon is green cheese, Matt thought, the cheese must be made from cream skimmed off the Milky Way. He hoped his mother could hear his thoughts.

Feeling giddy, Matt skipped down the path, almost bursting with joy. The gentle breeze was like his mother's breath, blowing through his hair.

The forest gave way to the forgotten square field that had become a meadow. The grass rippled in waves, and a grazing rabbit looked up from its nibbling, ears back. It didn't move as Matt walked by it to the tree stump he and his mother and his sister used to sit on. The rabbit pricked up its ears and continued to graze.

Matt sat and drew his knees up and hugged them to his chest. He wiggled his toes and shook his head.

This is where I want my ashes scattered, he thought. Here, where my mother and Jeannie and I spent some peaceful afternoons enjoying each other's company.

He looked around at this magical, forgotten field. The light from the moon made everything shimmer, as if the trees and grass were below the surface of a gently rippled pond. For the first time since the accident, Matt thought about swimming and how much he enjoyed racing. He pictured the pool where he'd swum that last meet. The water had looked so cold, yet it felt warm. Water is like that, Matt thought. It looks cold if *you* feel cold. And it looks warm if *you* feel warm. It's funny, Matt thought, but how water looks has nothing to do with its temperature.

Matt looked at the tall grass, swaying at his feet. The moonlight dimmed and Matt looked up. A long, wispy cloud was moving across the moon.

Loneliness is a little like feeling cold when you know the water is warm, Matt thought. I'm sometimes lonely in the middle of lots of people. Or, like now, I'm alone but I'm happy and close to everyone and everything.

There were times since his mother and sister died when he had felt very close to them — physically close. Tonight he felt that closeness stronger than ever. His mother was as far away as she could be — she was dead. And yet he felt that she was somewhere nearby. He thought about the times when she'd held him or sat next to him and he'd felt a million miles away.

These thoughts made him sad. I could have been nicer to her when she was alive, he thought. Next year, he vowed, I'll win all of my races for Mom and Jeannie.

But what if I lose one? Would that say something as bad as winning said something good?

I'll just race for myself, Matt decided, and swim my best. They would want it that way anyway, he thought. Matt looked up at the glimmering sky. *If Mom can hear my thoughts, she knows me better now, inside and out, than when she was alive. I wonder if any of it surprises her.*

He certainly had learned a lot about himself in the past four months. Not all of it was pleasant. But he'd grown. Matt felt years older and wiser. Things and people weren't as simple as they were before the accident. But he had to admit that people were more interesting and life seemed richer and more fascinating. It was as if he'd been watching a tiny black and white television all his life and now, suddenly, he was watching a giant color television.

And Scott had been right — time does heal some of the pain. And it made some of the hatred go away, too. For a while hatred had been to him like alcohol for Mr. Porter — a strong drug that he couldn't do without. But Scott had kept him posted on Mr. Porter. He was "off the juice," Scott said. Matt had kept Scott posted on his feelings. It had taken a while, but Matt was "off the hate." He didn't know what he'd do if he ever saw Mr. Porter again — but he didn't think he'd attack him.

Scott had been very patient with Matt. In fact, all of the Fletchers had been patient. Judy tried so hard to be perfect. She often fixed him his favorite meals, using his mother's recipes. She let him pack his sister's room. And she insisted that he decide to rent or sell his house. He chose to rent it. He thought he might want to live in it someday.

Jamie and he could hardly think of a time when they weren't brothers and sharing a room. They had some fights. But they were fiercely loyal to each other. And they were still best friends. Matt laughed harder with Jamie than anyone else. They ended almost every day by telling each other a joke. That evening Jamie giggled as they got into bed.

"What do you call a businessman whose store got hit by a tornado?" he asked Matt.

"What?" Matt asked back.

"A 'roofless' businessman. Get it?" Jamie laughed out loud. Matt laughed, too, making the bunk beds rock.

But Scott was the person Matt went to when he felt overwhelmed by the loss of his mother and sister. Matt had even asked Scott if he could call him "Father."

Scott thought about it a few moments. "I'm flattered, Matt," he said. "And I love you like a son. But when you say 'Father' I automatically think of your dad. He was a great guy, and I don't want to take his place, Matt." He paused. "And I don't think you will ever feel comfortable about calling Judy 'Mother.' She'll never be able to be your mother in the same way your real mother was. I just don't think it would be fair for you to call me 'Father' if you couldn't call her 'Mother.'

"But," Scott said, "if you don't mind, I'd be proud to call you 'Son.'"

Matt felt like crying. No man had ever called him "Son" and meant it. "I don't mind," he said.

Even though it had been a long time since the accident, Matt had never really said good-bye to his mother — or his sister. It was as if he kept putting it off, not really wanting to say it because that would make it final.

Matt watched the moon. It swelled as it sank toward the tips of the tree tops. For an instant the tiny branches arrested its sinking and balanced the moon delicately, like a balloon resting on a forest of crooked pins and needles. But the moon grew too heavy and it melted through the branches, glowing faint orange. It sank more quickly now and it flattened out and spread like orange paint spilled onto the horizon.

Matt felt so close to his mother and sister as he watched that he ached. The moon sank faster, farther, almost gone.

"Good-bye, Mom!"

Matt's voice sounded small in the meadow.

"Good-bye, Jeannie!"

The moon plunged below the horizon. The night sky darkened and the stars rejoiced, sparkling brighter than before.

Matt felt peaceful inside. Calm and peaceful with a little ache of sadness. He sighed and then yawned. His eyelids drooped and he felt very sleepy. Matt curled up on the stump. The breeze picked up for a moment and he listened to its faint whistle and rustle and moan. It seemed to say, "Goodnight, Matt."

Matt felt alone for the first time since he'd stepped outside. Peaceful, alone, and a little sad. He reached down and touched himself. It felt good. Matt didn't feel guilty about this glowing pleasure anymore. His mother would understand. And Jeannie probably touched herself too when she felt alone or sad. Matt closed his eyes and soon he fell asleep.

The sun bubbled up over the horizon, gathered itself into a ball, and shone into Matt's face. Matt opened his eyes and looked out at the meadow. He sat up stiffly, rubbing the sleep out of his eyes. He felt chilled. In the pale sunlight he felt funny sitting completely naked on a tree stump in the middle of a field surrounded by trees.

He jumped up from the stump and laughed as dew from the grass drenched his legs and feet. He did a little dance in front of the stump and then took off, full tilt, toward the path and home.

He ran along the path, feeling strong and nimble, through the forest and out into the Fletchers' backyard. He quickly looked around. A car was coming up the street, and Matt scurried up to the house and into the back door. He made his way through the house, listening for signs that someone might be up. The house was quiet.

Catlike, Matt crept up the stairs and into his room. Jamie was asleep. Matt crawled up into his bed.

He was home, in bed, before anybody was awake! It was

a grand, wonderful secret. Matt decided he would never tell anybody about the remarkable night in the field.

He never did. But the bottoms of his sheets, inside, were muddy. And when Judy asked about them, a few days later, Matt didn't even try to explain. He just shrugged his shoulders and smiled.

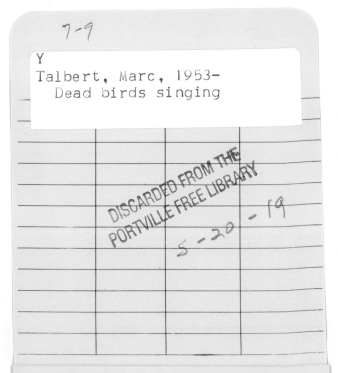